other books by
janet tashjian

The Gospel According to Larry
Vote for Larry
Multiple Choice
Tru Confessions

fault line

janet tashjian

HENRY HOLT and COMPANY

NEW YORK

Henry Holt and Company, LLC
Publishers since 1866
175 Fifth Avenue
New York, New York 10010
www.henryholtchildrensbooks.com

Henry Holt® is a registered trademark of Henry Holt and Company, LLC.
Copyright © 2003 by Janet Tashjian
All rights reserved.
Distributed in Canada by H. B. Fenn and Company Ltd.

Library of Congress Cataloging-in-Publication Data
Tashjian, Janet.
Fault line / Janet Tashjian.
p.   cm.
Summary: When seventeen-year-old Becky Martin, an aspiring comic,
meets Kip Costello, she is caught in a mentally
and physically abusive relationship.
[1. Comedians—Fiction. 2. Dating (Social customs)—Fiction.
3. Abused women—Fiction.] I. Title.
PZ7.T211135Fau 2003   [Fic]—dc21   2002038888

ISBN-13: 978-0-8050-8063-6 / ISBN-10: 0-8050-8063-5
1   3   5   7   9   10   8   6   4   2

First published in hardcover in 2003 by Henry Holt and Company
First paperback edition, 2006
Printed in the United States of America on acid-free paper.

For Christy

fault line

Take my life . . . please.

Laughter is one of the only things in life you can count on to bail you out of anything. Even when you're grief-stricken, shocked, or petrified, laughter can bring you back to that place deep inside that knows there's life beyond your pain. I remember the day I learned this in my bones: my uncle Danny had just died, and my mother had spent most of the morning sobbing at the kitchen table. I was maybe four at the time, feeling more helpless than usual. My father had brought up some extra chairs from the basement for all the relatives who would be coming in from out of town. I didn't notice when I sat on one that it was missing its cane seat. PLOP—I went right through the frame of the chair onto the floor. I didn't cry; I grinned—the shock of the fall was a welcome surprise from all the sadness. My mother burst into laughter at the sight of her little girl sprawled on the rug, smiling. Which of course made me fall through the chair again. And again. It was as if I had

5

waved a magic wand. Before my very eyes, she was transformed from a broken-hearted woman back into good old Mom. Because of my actions, because of *me*. Humor was something thunderous from the heavens, with a power to change things in an instant.

Of course, bottling something as formidable as lightning is a tricky thing. Trickier still to do it night after night. Most of the time when I'm onstage, I feel like an alchemist: mixing a little bit of this story, a slice of that detail to come up with a fresh and humorous *aha* for the crowd to enjoy. But sometimes you fall flat, with a joke so inert you want to hang your coat on it. Those nights, it's back to the drawing board, pure and simple.

Here's what I want more than anything: not to headline the Improv, not to join the cast of *SNL*. (Okay, you nailed me. OF COURSE I WANT THOSE THINGS. I'd be lying if I said I didn't.) But more than those—much more—I want to learn how to trust my instincts. It's the part of comedy I haven't gotten a handle on yet, although I work on those skills all the time. Where I intuitively come up with some thought on the spot that binds me and the audience together for a brief moment—I get goose bumps just thinking about it. During each performance, there's some connection with the audience, but I'm talking about the cathartic, spontaneous kind. The search for that link keeps me writing jokes, keeps me auditioning, keeps me hoping lightning can strike.

I'm like Ben Franklin in a storm, holding a kite, a key, and a jar.

Waiting to connect.

"I bombed last night," I told my friend Abby.

"The Bob Marley routine, I bet. Becky, it's just not *funny.*"

"I love that bit."

"There's no payoff."

"I was going for something different."

"Like what—audience narcolepsy?" Abby asked. "Tell the one about your mother hosting that drag-queen Tupperware party with Delilah. Now *that's* funny."

"I was aiming a little higher than Delilah demonstrating her version of the Tupperware burp."

"Too bad you weren't this funny last night," she said. "You would've killed."

Abby and I were closer than sisters—not that I knew what that was like, having only my six-year-old brother, Christopher, to compare her to. She and I met because our last names both begin with *M,* and we were assigned to the same homeroom every year. Sometime in junior high, we discovered our mutual love of comedy and old movies. She was gorgeous, I was quiet; we never would've hooked up on our own. It took something as random as a letter of the alphabet to forge a friendship this strong. Funny how that works.

But even after all these years, I still couldn't figure Abby out. She had a crude sense of humor—constantly pulling pranks, laughing at fart jokes—yet woke up at five o'clock every morning to meditate. She hated hanging out with a lot of people, yet craved a packed house. She loved to travel, yet refused to apply to colleges outside of San Francisco because she wanted to continue her practice at the local Zen Center. My best friend was an enigma even to me.

We grabbed two coffees and a booth for our usual round of Saturday catch-up at the local diner. We talked about how the comedy scene was slowly turning around (finally!). We wished we'd been born fifteen or twenty years earlier, when San Francisco was one of the top cities in the country to work, when Robin Williams performed to SRO crowds several nights a week. Back then, Margaret Cho had left home at sixteen to hit the road; now, at seventeen, we usually had to lie our way into the clubs. The Punch Line wouldn't even let us in without a parent—were they kidding? Because we were still learning, no gig was a waste, not even emceeing shows at the community center or Y. And—hope of hopes!—a scout for Conan or Letterman might spot us someday and ask us to perform.

Although the school year had just begun, the Saturday morning yak-fest was fast becoming our senior-year routine. It never got Abby and me an inch closer to playing bigger clubs, but it reassured us that we weren't wasting our time practicing into tape recorders and mirrors for nothing, that we actually might have a minuscule shot at being funny for a living.

We ordered two more coffees to go, then headed to Union Square for Saturday Ritual #2. For years our school had had a community service requirement for seniors. Most of the other students had volunteered in a church or homeless shelter, but not us. Because Abby had been going to the Zen Center since she was twelve, she talked one of the monks into signing off on our "outreach program."

Our idea—filtered through Abby's love of Zen and our mutual flair for the theatrical—was to get people to be more present, more *aware*. So we went to various locales in the city and flashed cards with Zen mottos at the people walking by: ARE YOU AWAKE? ARE YOU HERE OR SOMEWHERE ELSE? WAKE UP! And Abby's favorite, WHEREVER YOU GO, THERE YOU ARE. People usually either ignored us or thought we wanted money—we collected fifteen dollars our first time out—but once in a while someone really *got* it. Those people would look us in the eyes and smile, become more present in their day.

"This is so much better than calling out bingo numbers at the nursing home," Abby said.

"I'm almost convinced we *are* performing a service," I agreed. "That last guy shifted right in front of me."

"I keep telling you, you've got to come to the Center. A roomful of people meditating for hours." Abby flashed her card and a smile at a mother wheeling crying twins in a stroller. The poor woman looked like she didn't want to be present.

Maybe it was the beautiful fall weather or a very conscious neighborhood, but several other people really responded. An old man put down his groceries and asked us about our project; we ended up talking to him for twenty minutes.

After an hour and a half, we packed it in.

"You want to come to the movies with Kevin and me?" Abby asked.

Going to the movies was an opportunity I'd usually never say no to, but I had two papers to finish. Kevin was a nice guy Abby had met through her brother, Billy; I never felt like a fifth wheel joining them. I liked Kevin a lot but knew not to get too attached to the guys who stepped through the revolving door of Abby's affections.

I left Abby in Union Square and headed home. When a woman walked by me carrying a Chihuahua wearing a calico bonnet, I took out my notebook and logged the image for future use.

Ed Lynch from the next street over walked by too; he had graduated from my high school the year before. Even though we passed each other almost every day, he never bothered to nod or say hello. I had given up trying to be friendly months ago. It wasn't just Ed. When it came to most guys, it was as if I were wearing invisibility sunscreen. It's not that there was anything wrong with me—okay, maybe I was a bit on the uncoordinated side, too eager to please—but with most guys it seemed as if processing my presence wasn't worth their time.

Friends and family have always described me as two things: smart and funny. Never pretty, never interesting, just smart and funny. I wasn't complaining—those were necessary qualities for my chosen line of work—but it would be nice to at least *register* on the attractiveness scale once in a while.

Unlike Abby, I hadn't had a boyfriend since Peter last year, and even that was stretching the definition of boyfriend way past anything Webster would have recognized. I had better luck holding the attention of a roomful

of people in a comedy club than a guy—I couldn't decide
if that was good or just plain pathetic. Idea for a routine—
in my neighborhood growing up, I was everybody else's
invisible friend.

I looked at the card peeking out of my bag. ARE YOU
AWARE?

I finished the rest of the sentence in my mind. ARE
YOU AWARE THAT NO ONE IS AWARE OF YOU?

I scribbled a quick bit about Zen riddles in my notebook. Just because Abby wasn't going to use them in her
act didn't mean I couldn't give it a go. They'd be better
than the sex, drugs, and parents jokes that filled the sets
of most comics my age.

I smiled, thinking about the sign from last year's
comedy workshop that I'd hung over my desk at home:
IF LIFE GIVES IT TO YOU, USE IT.

Being in comedy was similar to working at a giant
recycling center—nothing went to waste.

13

When I first told my mother I wanted to hit the comedy scene, she flipped. Late nights, grades, alcohol, secondhand smoke—blah, blah, blah. It took two years of playing local parties and talent shows before she finally let me drag her to the Comedy Stop downtown. (One good thing about living in the city: I've grown up bopping around the many different neighborhoods, using public transportation, and always—always—gathering material.)

I started sneaking into teen open-mike nights at the local Jewish Community Center. I wasn't Jewish, so the first time I went, I pinned one of the shoulder pads from one of my mother's suits onto the back of my head for a yarmulke. I found out when I got there, of course, that the men usually wore the yarmulkes. The woman who helped me unpin the shoulder pad took pity and let me run through my routine anyway. It was my first time on-stage, but I strode to the microphone with confidence.

All the awards I'd won in school for academic excellence paled in comparison to the scattered applause of a handful of kids sitting in a Nob Hill gym at four o'clock on a Sunday afternoon.

I was fifteen years old and hooked.

A few of the clubs used to let us sneak in underage, until the city clamped down on the drinking laws. So for almost three years—God bless her—my mother sat in smoky clubs and watched me perform. (Except when I auditioned; I was always so nervous, I made her wait outside.) On open-mike nights like this one, the quality of material could be iffy at best. Mom never complained.

When Mom couldn't go, she sent her assistant to be the adult who accompanied us. Delilah had been with us for years. She was a tall, black, athletic drag queen who was my uncle Danny's boyfriend up until the end. Uncle Danny contracted AIDS back in the early eighties; his illness brought us here from Seattle. Mom and Delilah comforted Uncle Danny through his pain, then comforted each other when he finally died. Mom and Dad said we were staying in San Francisco because of the weather and the career opportunities, but even then I knew Mom couldn't bear the thought of leaving the city where her only brother was buried. When Delilah's travel agency went under a few years later, Mom hired her as a full-time Jill-of-all-trades. I never knew Delilah's

real name or saw her out of costume; she flipped if anyone referred to her as "he." She was known around the
Castro for her impersonations of TV moms. When she
walked down the street as Carol Brady, people hounded
her for autographs.

Mom sat down in the back of the club, ordered herself a beer, and told me to have fun. I headed to the lobby
to wait with Abby.

"Are you doing the bit about the stuttering tele-
marketers?" she asked.

"Nah. This is my new Leap Year set. I'm not sure it's
ready yet. What are you doing?"

Abby put out her cigarette at the bar. "My I-hate-the-
Olympics bit."

One of my favorites.

"Hey, let's scrap our routines and just wing it," Abby
suggested.

"Yeah, right." I kept walking.

She blocked my path. "I'm serious. Like that Improv
class we took last year at the Learning Center."

"Half of those skits we did were horrible," I said.

"The other half were brilliant. Come on—BE HERE
NOW, remember?"

"No way. There's too much at stake."

"There's *nothing* at stake," she said. "The only people
here are tourists and freaks like us."

I told her not everyone was Paula Poundstone, having impromptu dialogues with the audience all night. Abby barely listened; she'd heard my excuses before. I knew sooner or later I'd have to let go and trust my instincts more, but it scared the life out of me. Standing onstage in front of people? No problem. Winging it without a script? Trusting in my gut that I'd know what to do? Problem. Big Problem.

Rick, the manager, approached the mike.

He'd owned the Comedy Stop for twenty years, had seen all the heavy hitters come and go and go and go. . . . His stories of Jon Stewart showing up to encourage the newcomers kept all of us eyeing the door in anticipation. Rick was shorter than I and wore the same Buzzcocks T-shirt every night. The fact that he encouraged us and kept us on the open-mike list made Abby and me overlook the fact that we'd never been paid a cent. Because we valued his friendship—and the experience—we never mocked his lack of wardrobe in our sets.

I leaned against the wall and watched Abby perform. I knew most of her routines as well as my own. She riffed on the Olympic judges, the bobsled team, then ad-libbed with a woman drinking a martini at the front table. They went back and forth about the closing ceremonies until the woman's friends were in hysterics. Abby was great at thinking on her feet, one of the best.

As the audience applauded, I performed my preshow warm-up—jumping up and down like a pogo stick, shaking out my arms and legs. I set my tape recorder on a stack of boxes and pressed "record." I'd been taping all my shows since Mr. Ellin's comedy-writing class last year. He said, "Learn from your audience; they'll tell you everything you need to know about your act." Since then, I analyzed every show—where the audience stayed with me, where they drifted off. And most important, what I could do differently next time. It was a comedy postmortem I kept in my current notebook; I looked forward to the ritual in a masochistic kind of way.

Before Abby came off, I searched through my bag for the Zen cards. ARE YOU PRESENT? WHAT DO YOU SEE?

Hopefully people laughing.

I handed Abby my bag, watched Rick introduce me, then took the stage.

~

Some snippets from my set:

"Hi, I'm Becky and I'm bissextile."

A few hoots.

"I wish it were half as exciting as it sounds. It just means I was born on a Leap Year."

Dead air. Not good.

"When I was a kid, those February 29 birthdays—the

REAL birthdays—THOSE were the only years I didn't feel like a fraud. My mother worked that frog theme like a pro. Frog napkins, frog plates, even a ridiculous chocolate cake shaped like a frog. As if frogs are the only things that can leap—couldn't we have based one of those parties on a ballerina or gazelle? Talk about feeding into my low self-esteem . . ."

A few chuckles—probably Mom. I knew this set wasn't ready.

"The bad news is that on my last birthday I was only four and three-quarters; the good news is, that's just about the mental age of most of the guys at my school."

Laughter—finally.

"I wish this whole one-in-four concept applied to losing weight . . . if a bag of Oreos contained a quarter of the calories, now THAT would be a good thing."

Polite laughter. Worse than none at all.

"But I want to know why a groundhog gets his own day every year and I don't. It isn't fair. I actually started a Leap Year support group in the basement of our church. I call it our three-step program."

Mild applause. At this rate, I'll be lucky to be performing on cruise ships.

"Thanks—good night."

NOTES TO SELF:

● Add to Leap Year set—"During elections, my vote only counts for a quarter of the items on the ballot"—no, not there yet.

● Don't follow Abby.

● They're already planning the stupid harvest dance. Why does everything at school have to be based on couples?

● New idea—a riff on rap fairy tales—Little Red Riding-in-the-Hood, Rapunzel with hair extensions—could be funny (or at least better than my Leap Year set).

My parents' career paths couldn't have been more different. Mom ran her own law firm; Dad was a waiter. Not at the local greasy spoon, but a professional, been-doing-it-for-twenty-years kind of waiter. He worked in the Ritz-Carlton Dining Room, arguably the most prestigious restaurant in a city known for its cuisine. None of that "Hi, I'm Bennett. I'll be your waiter tonight" kind of stuff—just silent, impeccable service, anticipating the customers' whims even before they knew they needed anything. Our family had lived on Dad's income quite adequately for years while Mom was starting her practice. One of her first clients was an unknown local software company. She worked for next to nothing in the beginning, then made the intuitive decision to get paid in stock when they went public. She sealed the deal with the CEO right there at the Ritz while my father waited on them. Other women might have met their client somewhere else or not acknowledged their husband was a waiter, but not Mom. She introduced the CEO to Dad over drinks, and when she stuck a pen in the CEO's hand after coffee, my father dusted away the crumbs from the table to make room for the contract. Mom's one-woman law firm sure could have used the money up-front, but Mom's always been big on risk taking. She watched the stock go from three dollars to sixteen to ninety to two hundred, finally selling her shares at two hundred thirty-nine. Mom gave half the credit to Dad, saying his recommendation of the stuffed Dover sole clinched the deal.

This is not to say we *lived* rich. In fact, Mom was so frugal, most of the time you'd think we were bordering on broke. She still dyed her hair in the kitchen sink and refused to buy us Christmas presents until the sales kicked in on December 26. We stayed in the same two-family we'd lived in before her windfall. The biggest differences were that we no longer had tenants upstairs, and we now had a large library. My parents had spent a month of weekends installing mahogany bookcases along all four walls of the double parlor upstairs. They worked on it for weeks, finally filling both rooms floor-to-ceiling with books. (The stacks and stacks of them piled around the house had been adding up, I guess.) The lustrous shelves and accompanying ladders were the only visible proof of my mother's stock deal.

Mom constantly touted the importance of earning

your own living; the only reason I never argued with her was that I loved my two part-time jobs. I'd been working at the Goodwill store downtown for more than a year. Some of my best material had come from the ridiculous stuff people brought in as donations, not to mention our quirky clientele. I learned more about the city there than I ever could by studying the daily newspaper.

I'd only had my other job for a month, but I already couldn't imagine life without it. When I saw the ad at our local diner, I tore the flyer off the bulletin board so no one else could respond. One of the local tourist companies ran a bus trip that highlighted all the famous movie spots in San Francisco. Since my mom and I were movie freaks and I needed all the "stage" experience I could get, the job was tailor-made for me. I thought I scared the guy on the interview when I came up with esoteric examples only a handful of tourists might want to see. (When I mentioned Francis Ford Coppola's vineyard up north, I wasn't sure if I came off more as a stalker or a fan.) I got the job anyway. So once a week, I donned my standard-issue navy blazer and helped Mr. Perez lead a busload of tourists through the cinematic history of the city.

Even before I landed the job, the walls of my room were completely covered with movie posters I'd collected over the years. Abby and I had recently started adding voice balloons to the mouths of our favorite characters, letting Hannibal Lecter or Forrest Gump test our latest material. Once in a while I'd find an attempt at a joke pinned to one of the posters closest to the floor. The scrawled handwriting and potty jokes always gave Christopher away.

Dad was trimming the hedges so they wouldn't drape over the sidewalk while Mom planted the fall bulbs as if someone were standing behind her with a stopwatch. She tamped down the soil with her daisy-print gloves and told me my boss had called.

"Which one?"

"Mr. Perez. He said to tell you they've decided to add *American Graffiti* to the tour."

"I can't believe he finally took my suggestion."

"How do you do a movie tour of San Francisco without that classic?" Mom asked. "It should've been one of the first on their list."

"You'll be running the company soon," my father told me between snips.

When the cordless phone rang, I picked it up from the lawn. It was Abby with Ritual #17—testing out a new joke.

"How about this?" she asked. "My boyfriend's so cheap,

when we go to Kentucky Fried Chicken, he licks *other* people's fingers."

"Gross, but funny. Especially since Kevin wouldn't be caught dead there."

"We broke up."

"What happened?" I sat down on the front steps to take in this new information.

"We just hit a dead end," she said.

"But you've been together almost three months."

"Time to move on."

Her cavalier attitude in the boyfriend department was yet another mysterious quality of my best friend. Long-term, short-term, serious, or casual, no relationship was ever a big deal for Abby. She then went into Best Friend Ritual #38—deconstructing the latest *SNL* show bit by bit. I tried to keep up with her as she analyzed several Weekend Update jokes, but I couldn't stop thinking about Kevin. They had seemed so happy together. I knew I'd never get any scoop from Abby—the present interested her much more than the past—but still. . . . Couldn't they have tried harder to make it work? Were things bad enough to throw the whole relationship away? I asked again for details, but she shrugged off my questions as irrelevant.

As usual, I was putting more effort into analyzing my best friend's relationships than she was.

Life is what you're stuck with
while you're waiting to have one.

Write jokes.

Write school papers.

Write jokes in the margins of my school papers.

Same old routine.

There was one piece of excitement at my movie-tour job, however. While the other tourists were taking photos of the street where they filmed the famous car chase in *Bullitt,* an eighty-two-year-old man named Hector Santos had a quiet heart attack in the back of the bus. Mr. Perez dealt with the paramedics while I was forced to converse with and comfort the crowd for forty-five minutes. Not fun. We heard the next day that Hector was okay. Thank God. (Imagine: The last thing you see on earth is Barbra Streisand's apartment in *What's Up, Doc?*)

I continued to hone my Leap Year set; it was almost beginning to be funny. Mom was so used to hearing it, she actually sat at Rick's and did paperwork during most of my act. Delilah had OD'd on my jokes too; she burned up her cell sitting at the bar.

I finally nailed the three-step joke: *"We Leap Year people are cured way before the boozers. We only have three steps."*

Biggest laugh I'd had in months.

"Bravo! Bravo!" my mother said when Abby and I returned to the table.

"Actually, Ms. M., when you're applauding a woman, it's *brava!*" Abby said.

"Becky, why do you hang out with such a know-it-all?"

"It gives me a break from doing all the thinking," I answered.

Abby pulled her knit cap farther down over her eyes. "Longest laugh I got lasted two seconds."

"Two seconds is huge. Besides, your LPM was almost five."

My mom asked what I was talking about.

"Laughs per minute. We used to get three, now we're up to five."

"I didn't realize you two were getting so scientific about this."

"Next time bring your periodic table," Abby said.

"Does she have to bring the chair too?" I asked. "You'd think that would be included in the cover charge."

Abby rapped the table in a drum roll. (One of the

downfalls of hanging out with comics: we never know when to quit.)

"That bit about the three steps," Mom said, "much better now."

"Thanks, but it's not like it was wall-to-wall laughs or anything."

"Oh, and I've been thinking about this. You had *one* frog-themed party, missy—one! That stupid cake took me all day to make!" Mom got up from the table. "I've got to work tomorrow. You two coming?"

"It's only nine-thirty," I said. "Can we stay?"

She finally caved. "Delilah can take you home later. I'll grab a cab." She searched through her purse for what seemed like an eternity. I finally reached into the pocket of my jeans and took out a crumpled ten.

"Ms. M., you are the most sorry-ass millionaire I know," Abby said.

"That's because I'm an attorney. It's not necessarily the same thing."

Abby grinned; she loved teasing my mother about everything—her job, old movies, her politics.

After Mom left, Abby and I ordered two more sodas and kicked back to catch the other acts. While some woman actually tried to get laughs as a ventriloquist—*hel-lo?*—I noticed a cute guy at one of the back tables. He had a roll of paper towels and was writing furiously, his head only inches from the paper. He looked like he was writing to save his life. I asked Abby if she knew him, but she'd never seen him before either.

As usual, she took things into her own hands. "Hey, Mr. Bounty! What are you doing?"

It looked as if the interruption had disoriented him. He smiled awkwardly, tucked the roll of towels under his arm, and pulled up a chair at our table. He told us he was working on a new set. One of us.

He was adorable—messy dark curls, deep-blue eyes, tall and thin, our age. My type, anybody's type.

He nodded in my direction. "Liked the bit about the three steps."

"You're the second person to say that, so I guess I'll keep it in."

"But the other person was your mother, so that doesn't really count," Abby added.

Abby and I hadn't gotten into a who-gets-him-first? contest since junior high, and I hoped we wouldn't get into one now. Mostly because she always won.

"You want some feedback?" he asked. "Just say no if you don't."

"No, I do. Desperately." It was true; I always wanted to hear everything about my sets, good *and* bad. It was the only way to improve.

"You've got some good setups, but you've got to punch up your payoffs. Get them a bit tighter."

I asked him what he meant.

"Well, like 'Since I was born on Leap Year, I don't get a full vote on election day.' The punchline isn't strong enough. Instead say something like 'My vote counts less than yours, but then again, *nobody*'s vote counted during the Bush/Gore election.'"

"That's much better," I said. "And I worked on that one for hours."

He shrugged, almost embarrassed. I pointed to the paper towels and asked what he was working on.

"A routine about my mother's antique shop—the people who come in, the yard sales she goes to, the junk that people think is valuable."

"Could be funny," Abby said.

"That's the plan."

"You got a problem with notebooks?" I asked.

"The whole killing trees thing is too depressing."

"But aren't paper towels made from—"

"Yeah, but at least when I'm finished, I can use them to clean up my apartment."

Abby's goal to get her own place as soon as possible reared its head, as usual. "You have your own apartment?"

"Not really. My mom and I live over her antique shop in this rent-controlled building in Noe Valley. My rooms have a separate entrance."

He was talking to Abby but looking my way—a welcome confidence booster, believe me.

Rick gave us the high sign from the bar.

"Got to go," Mr. Bounty said. "I'm on."

"Now?" we shouted. This guy's casual attitude made Abby and me seem like major stress cases. He left his paper towels on our table and headed toward the stage.

Abby picked up the roll and skimmed through the scrawled handwriting.

"Hey, that's private." I yanked the roll away from her.

"Oh, like you don't want to know."

I tucked the roll onto the chair beside me and focused on the stage.

"Ladies and gentlemen!" Rick said. "A real find—Kip Costello!"

Abby's head whipped in my direction. "Kip? You can't go out with a guy named Kip!"

"Who says I'm going to go out with him?"

"Becky and Kip. That's worse than Barbie and Ken. Blech!"

I ignored her and checked out Kip as he began his set. He wore jeans and a green T-shirt under an unbuttoned oxford shirt—like he had respect for the audience but didn't want to put too much effort into planning what to wear. (Unlike Abby and me, who still made a federal case out of the wardrobe issue.)

Timing and pacing are two of the hardest things to get right in comedy, but Kip had both areas down. He built up slowly and by the end of his ten minutes, the audience was with him all the way. The bit about his grandfather confusing anthrax with Amtrak had the crowd howling.

Me? I wished I had a videocamera to capture this great set on film so I could watch it again and study every joke. Well, not just the jokes. . . . But whether or not Kip and I would ever see each other again, he was a great addition to our humble comedy scene, no doubt about it.

Afterward Kip made his way back to our table.

"You were great," I said. "Why haven't we seen you before?"

"We moved here from Napa this year," Kip said. "I've been driving out to the suburbs to hone my act before I finally got up the nerve to perform in the city. Afraid of failure, I guess."

"Aren't we all."

"My last two gigs were at a Chinese restaurant and a bowling alley. This is a big upgrade."

The three of us talked nonstop for the rest of the night. About everything, from Kip's high school across town to the bawdiness of Mel Brooks. We bitched about people getting into stand-up just to showcase themselves for a sitcom and about how difficult the business still was for women. Between performers we continued a cut-throat debate—was Comedy Central the best or worst thing to happen to stand-up? (Abby and I went back and forth several times; Kip stuck with an emphatic "worst!")

Thankfully, this wasn't the typical one-upmanship routine that passed for conversation in the comedy crowd. I liked joking around as much as the next person, but sometimes you just wanted to talk. Especially when the other person was as funny and intense as Kip appeared to be.

Now, I am a connoisseur of details—it's a job requirement. And here's the tiny detail that just slayed me. As he spoke, I noticed the round transparent sizing sticker stuck to the pocket of Kip's green T-shirt. He obviously hadn't noticed the circle containing the bold black *L*, but I did. I loved the fact that I knew something about him no one else knew, including him.

I checked my watch often, knowing Delilah would be ready to leave at eleven o'clock sharp. She was—in all her *Bewitched* glory. I don't know how she did it, but her hair—unlike my long, unruly mane—was always completely in place.

"Let's go, honeys. It's a school night." She glanced over at Kip. "And who is this handsome young thing?"

I introduced them.

"Was she your nanny when you were young?" Kip asked me as we walked to the door. "Because *that* would be a routine."

I said she took care of my little brother when she wasn't driving the rest of the family all over town or scheduling my mother's meetings. Then I held out my hand and told Kip it had been fun hanging out with him.

"Then we should do it again, right?"

I took the paper towels from him and gently unrolled them to a new square. I wrote down my home and cell numbers. When I looked up, he was smiling at me.

"You know what you remind me of?" he asked.

This was all Abby needed to hear. "Here we go," she said.

He ignored her. "Cinnamon. Anyone ever tell you that?"

"I think I would have remembered that one."

"The bronze skin, the freckles, the reddish hair. Cinnamon all the way."

"Yeah, she's a real Spice Girl." Abby rolled her eyes so hard I thought the ceiling fan might fall to the floor.

Kip continued nonetheless. "You know that Neil Young song, 'Cinnamon Girl'? That should be your nickname."

I could feel the inner cinnamon rising to my cheeks. "Kind of a long nickname, don't you think?"

Abby decided to expand her repertoire to include impersonations—this one of a wet blanket. "You don't know her well enough to give her a nickname," she said.

I had thought that too, of course, but was too flattered to say.

He grinned and headed to the door. "That can change." He waved the paper towel like a flag of surrender. "I'll call you."

Abby could barely contain her disdain when he left. "What a phoney. And I'm not saying that because he picked you instead of me."

"Of course you are, but that's okay. Admit it, his punchline about the voting was much better than mine."

"So he's funny, so what?"

"You're not being very Zen." My trump card line with Abby; it *always* shut her up.

Almost always.

"You will never hear from him again," she said. "I guarantee it."

I tried to construct an emotional barrier between my inner excitement and her outer negativity. Needless to say, Delilah loved the drama and insisted on hearing every last detail on the drive back.

Later at home, I went downstairs to shut off the lights. I opened the cabinet next to the stove and spun the lazy Susan around till I spotted the tin of cinnamon. When I finally figured out how to open the canister, I sprinkled a little on my finger and inhaled—dark and exotic. I licked the dab off my finger and was surprised at the pungent taste. I guess that's why my mother always mixed it with sugar before she sprinkled it on our apple slices when we were kids. I'd gone out with only a few guys over the years, but none of them were creative or interesting enough to come up with a nickname for me, never mind during our first meeting. Not that I would be going out with Kip—in this lifetime, at least. I shut off the kitchen lights and told my mind to stop racing.

It was crazy to even think about him; he was probably a giant flirt who practiced this routine every night. As far as I knew, he could have a spice rack full of nicknames for every girl in town. The last thing I needed was to be competing with hot girls like Clove and Nutmeg.

This guy had taken my freckles, my reddish hair—qualities I'd been embarrassed about for years—and turned them into things to praise. Maybe he was a magician, not a comic at all.

Interesting, handsome, creative. Liked *me*?

I told myself to forget about him.

He was obviously too good to be true.

NOTES TO SELF:

● Kip's election joke—tied to political events—
learn from this.
● A bit about nicknames?
● Finish lab report for Friday—get notes from
Charlie—like he took any.
● If a person is a part-time bandleader, is he a
semi-conductor? Might work in Silicon Valley.
● Dig through my files in case I run short again.
● Work on that bit about having a father who goes
to work in a tuxedo—hopefully Dad won't mind.
● If Kip doesn't call—when he doesn't call—maybe
run into him next Friday night at the club. . . .

From the Paper Towel Dialogues of
Kip Costello

Did I blow it?

Come on too strong?

What if she hates Neil Young, hates that song, hates nicknames?

Could I just shut up and listen for once?

There's such a fine line between knowing what you're doing and looking like a giant dope. I hate those guys who make it look so easy; every time I try to act that way, I sound like some kind of weirdo on a bad TV commercial. Suppose I call her and she says no . . . ? But we had fun; she'd probably say yes to at least <u>one</u> date. It's been six months since we moved here; I've got to jump in sometime. Might be worth breaking open a fresh roll and writing down a few things to talk about so I don't seem like such a knucklehead.

I'm thinking about making a crib sheet with conversational topics to impress a girl I just met— does it get any more pathetic than that?

Thankfully Abby was wrong.

Kip called the next night.

And the next and the next . . .

Our first date: the restaurant was full, with an hour-and-a-half wait. Recipe for disaster, right? Instead we got take-out chicken and noodles, drove up to Twin Peaks, and ate dinner overlooking the city. The movie we wanted to see was sold out—thank God, he loves movies too—so we walked around the Mission admiring the architecture until we came across two beat-up armchairs someone had left on the curb for trash. We dragged them to the corner, where we sat on the sidewalk pretending we had remote controls, clicking them at people as they walked by. Kip's running commentary was clever and original; my lines were nowhere near as funny, although I did interject the occasional zinger.

Date two: Kip picked me up at Goodwill to go to the movies. He listened to me complain about the two-station radio my boss kept on all day with right-wing talk shows. A few days later when I came into work, the radio was gone and an old but still-working cd player was in its place. Harold, my boss, told me some guy skateboarded into the store and *had* to have the old radio, trading it for the cd player. Listening to the Flaming Lips instead of Rush Limbaugh greatly improved the quality of my work day, believe me.

For the first time in my life, I didn't feel like an uncoordinated loser. Usually when I couldn't open a Ziploc bag or cd, I felt like the most incompetent person on the planet. Kip actually found my deficiency in the fine-motor-skills department endearing and smiled as he helped me conquer the many inanimate objects that confounded me throughout the day.

I felt comfortable around him. So when my mother suggested Kip join us for dinner a few weeks into the relationship, I thought it might be fun.

My father had spent enough time in the Ritz-Carlton's kitchen to absorb the most intricate cooking challenges. While Kip and I sipped seltzers at the counter, Dad steamed a basket of artichokes, extracting the tender hearts for dipping in lemon butter. Before we even looked for them, linen napkins and tiny forks appeared beside our plates. Lucky for me, Mom reined herself in from using her cross-examination skills and kept the conversation polite.

"How did you like growing up in Napa?" she asked Kip.

"It was kind of weird," he answered. "Very touristy, with more spas than kids. But beautiful. Harvest time especially."

He went into a routine about the town's population—a strange mix of upper-middle-class and migrant workers. He compared the hardworking grape pickers to his snooty neighborhood friends, finishing up with a raucous *West Side Story* school dance scenario. My mother actually had to wipe the tears from her eyes.

Kip smiled at me as if to say, "See? This is easy. There was nothing to be worried about." I squeezed his hand under the table.

My mother gazed around the kitchen, then jumped up and down like a two-year-old. "Have I mentioned that I *love* being married to someone who cooks?" She helped my father bring the food to the table. Butterflied leg of lamb, braised fennel, curried couscous, and roasted asparagus.

"Please tell me you don't eat like this every night," Kip said.

"Every night Dad's home," I answered.

Mom called Christopher down for dinner. "On my nights, it's purely mac and cheese."

Christopher finally came to the table, toting his usual stack of paperbacks in his Scooby-Doo pillowcase. He'd been reading since he was four and claimed the two bottom shelves in the library as his own. He was now in a serious Captain Underpants phase, and several times during dinner my mom had to put the kibosh on his colorful language. I was crazy about Christopher but had to admit he was one weird little guy. He silently checked out Kip as we ate.

~

After dinner, Mom dragged Kip downstairs to show him her yard-sale video collection.

"Charlie Chaplin, Buster Keaton, and Harold Lloyd," Kip said. "No wonder Becky's funny."

"Becky was funny before she saw these," Mom said. "Besides, physical comedy's not her thing."

"Albert Brooks—my hero," I said.

"I'll drink to that." Kip clinked my glass in a toast.

I told him about my family's preferred video activity—watching movies with the sound off, playing a cd in the background at the same time, looking for scenes that made sense.

"Like the urban legend about *The Wizard of Oz* and *Dark Side of the Moon*," Kip said. "They're synchronized perfectly—until the cd ends, of course."

"That one's a classic," Mom said. "But it's more fun coming up with originals."

"*Citizen Kane* and *Led Zeppelin IV* is my favorite," I said.

"Hmmmm." Kip flipped through the stacks of videos. "How about *Singin' in the Rain* with *The Eminem Show*?"

Yet another reason why I was really beginning to like this guy.

"An inspired choice," Mom said. "Next time you're here, let's watch it."

When I was going out with Peter, I don't think he said two sentences to my mother, and even then I believe she had to remove them from his mouth with forceps. Maybe it was from all the stage experience, but Kip seemed more confident and secure.

When I came back into the room with coffee, my mom was asking Kip about the most embarrassing subject possible—his future.

"I'm applying to a few different schools," he answered. "But I'm also thinking about taking some time off to work on my act."

"Hmmmm."

I offered coffee in an effort to distract my mother from her mission.

She ignored me and plunged ahead. "College is so important. Becky's applying to schools with a few comedy and performing classes, but school's the operative word, not comedy."

"Well, if I had her grades, I'd be applying everywhere too."

"Your grades aren't good?"

"Mom! Why don't you ask him what he got on his SATs while you're at it?"

She looked at him expectantly.

"Kidding! I was kidding," I said.

She smiled. "So was I, Becky. Lighten up!"

Kip finally laughed; I did too. An eternity later, Mom picked up her cup and left the room.

"Sorry about that," I told Kip.

"No, she's right. That's important stuff." But something in his voice had shifted, and even my best material couldn't get it back. After his coffee, he said he had to study for a test and would call me tomorrow.

I went back to the kitchen, stood in the doorway, and watched my parents. Kip had kissed me good night on the porch, but here were Mom and Dad really getting into it.

"Do you mind?" I asked.

"Oh, come on," Mom said. "You've seen this a hundred times before."

"And it makes me sick every time." I cut myself a left-over slice of chocolate torte. "Well, what do you think?"

"He loved the lamb," Dad said.

"Besides his eating habits."

"He seems quite nice," Dad continued. "More mature than Peter."

"Peter was a dope," I said. "Three months of my life down the drain."

Thankfully neither of my parents brought up the fact that Peter had been the one to break up with me. I wanted to hear about how great Kip was, how smart and well-mannered, how funny his ideas were about our video night. The best I got was this:

"I bet Kip's act is good," Mom said. "He's very facile with words."

"I bring home a new boyfriend—"

"Is that what he is? I thought you two just started seeing each other."

"Whatever, a new person for you to meet, and all you have to say is 'he's facile with words'? There's not even another person on the planet who would use the word 'facile' in a sentence!"

"I'm sure this'll end up in one of your routines. Use it. You have my blessing."

I went upstairs before they started going at it again.

Mom's interrogation of Kip notwithstanding, the night had been a success. (Of course, compared to Dad catching Peter sneaking into the liquor cabinet to steal a bottle of rum, anything short of disaster could be counted on the plus side.)

My mind raced toward the year ahead—a fledgling career, a new boyfriend, graduation, college. The possibilities seemed endless.

But one item on my list of options seemed necessary, required.

Kip.

Pure and simple. I needed him as much as I wanted to stand onstage and make people laugh. As much as I hoped to make a career out of it.

That much.

Maybe even more.

NOTES TO SELF:

● Stop procrastinating and apply to schools already!

● Rumor—new club opening downtown? Check it out.

● Don't be nervous about meeting Kip's mom.

● Idea for movie tour—love stories set in San Francisco—Serendipity? No, too lame. Harold and Maude? Much better.

● Don't be so wimpy with hecklers.

● Finally broke through on that joke about the vegetarian refusing to eat animal crackers. Kip is brilliant!

● Muzzle Mom.

From the Paper Towel Dialogues of
Kip Costello

Her parents seemed okay. I mean, her father cooking a leg of lamb? Put a leg of lamb in <u>my</u> father's hand and he would have tried to club my mother with it. Dad was such a Neanderthal, the leg of lamb actually might have been a natural for him. Hey—a bit about caveman accessories—could be good.

I couldn't tell if her mom was trying to make me feel like a loser or if I felt like one on my own. A little intense, or what? God, I was sweating bullets, trying not to appear like Mr. Lowest Percentile. But Becky just shines; she's funny and smart and beautiful—like the skin box of Crayolas—all peach and brown and tan. I don't want to scare her away by moving too fast. Hopefully her mom will let Becky off the leash soon so she can check out my place. Now, that'll be a day when I won't mind things moving a little faster.

My boyfriend and I are in our own
little world. But it's okay—
they know us here.

If Abby and I averaged five laughs per minute, that ratio was *nothing* compared to the number of e-mails, IMs, and phone calls that passed between Kip and me over the next several weeks. My mom refrained from commenting on my immersion, losing it only when I jumped up from the table to answer the phone for the second time during dinner.

When I got out of school, Kip was there.

When I finished my shift at Goodwill, Kip was there.

Even when he wasn't there, he was there.

And he *sang.* All the time, softly enough not to bother people, but enough to serve as background music for everything we did. Driving in his truck, waiting in line for coffee—these experiences were transformed into events worthy of a soundtrack.

I was suddenly someone whose conversation was sprinkled with "My boyfriend and I did this" and "My boyfriend and I did that." If I were listening to someone else talk this way, I would've been forced to whip out the duct tape. As much as my own gushing made me sick, I was happy.

I was dying to see Kip's place, so when I finally had an afternoon that wasn't filled with either of my two jobs, the yearbook, or homework, he took me there.

When we entered the antique store downstairs, an old-fashioned bell announced our arrival. The large space was filled with homey furniture, lamps, and linens. A woman my mom's age dashed across the store to greet us.

"It's so nice to finally meet you, Becky. Please call me Alex."

"Her real name is Carol," Kip said. "But she thinks Alexandra is more classy for business."

"That's not true, and you know it." But she beamed at him as if he were the wittiest guy in the world. She then hurried us over to a loveseat in the corner of the main room. After depositing us there, she buzzed back with a platter of cheese, then ran off to get some tea.

"Does she always move this fast?" I whispered.

Kip tossed a cube of cheese into his mouth. "Makes the Road Runner look like he's on Valium."

I reached for my notebook.

"No way," Kip said. "Looney Tunes characters with substance abuse problems—that one's mine."

"Okay, but I'm warning you, if you don't use it soon, I'm stealing it."

He tossed a piece of cheese at me; I opened my mouth and caught it just in time.

When Alex finally sat down, I noticed the resemblance to Kip—the dimple on the left cheek, the curly dark hair. Her fingers strummed on her lap, her foot tapped. It was amazing that someone with her physical energy chose to spend her life in antiques. After twenty minutes of conversation, she told Kip she needed the truck to make a few deliveries. He helped her carry two dressers outside. If we hadn't been there, I bet she would have strapped them to her back and carried them out herself.

After she left, Kip locked up the shop.

"Since my brother, Zach, got married, it's just us. Mom works harder than anyone I know."

"She seems great."

"She went through a lot with my father, but things are much better now. We're actually a pretty normal family—*relatively* speaking."

I groaned at the pun.

He pulled me toward him and kissed me. Then he led me upstairs to an adjoining unit with a separate entrance. "This part of the building is mine. I have to admit, it's pretty great."

I stepped inside and was immediately dumbstruck. The rooms had all the beauty of the antique store downstairs, but with a more casual touch. A long pine table lined one wall; on another, an armoire distressed with just the right amount of whitewashed blue paint. From every angle, unusual pieces caught my eye—tall tin canisters full of bamboo stalks, a barbershop chair in the kitchen, a basket of billiard balls on the coffee table, Batman TV trays.

"Did you do this?" I finally stammered. "If so, my advice is to quit comedy immediately and go into decorating full-time." I faced him squarely. "Oh . . . I get it. This is too good to be true. You're gay."

He laughed, then explained that most of the pieces were part of his mother's rotating inventory. "I walked in a few weeks ago, and my bureau was gone. She's a mercenary—if someone wants to buy, she's selling."

Talk about a hotbed of material. I made a mental note for a bit about Martha Stewart in a catfight with an older woman from Provence, fighting over antique linens.

"Our old house in Napa was great too," he said. "Maybe sometime we can drive up there. It's less than two hours, but a world away from the city."

Future plans. We. Good signs.

I pointed to a closed door next to the kitchen. "What's in here?"

"That's the pantry. It's kind of a mess."

When he opened the door, I burst out laughing.

Piles of dirty laundry, stacks of magazines, and broken hockey sticks overflowed into the hallway.

"You weren't supposed to see this," Kip said. "I didn't want you to think I was a slob."

"I'm actually relieved. This is much more normal."

He grabbed handfuls of clothes and threw them back into the room. I took the magazines and tossed them next to the couch.

We admired our handiwork. "Much better," Kip said.

I suddenly noticed the back wall of the pantry was covered with paper towel racks, maybe ten of them. The rods were full of paper towels, all covered in Kip's black cursive.

"I sit in here and go through all my material. It works for me."

I touched the trailing end of the closest roll. "Do you mind?"

He nodded for me to go ahead.

After a few minutes, the hurried words became clear. A routine about special effects in the movies, a piece about his grandmother not being able to find her dentures. Rolls and rolls of Kip talking to an imaginary audience.

"It's like studying your mind," I said.

He reached out and ran his fingers through my tangled hair.

"My hair," I said. "It's always such a mess."

"What are you talking about? It's great."

"I'm so bad with it," I babbled. "I wish I were one of those people who could French braid or tie it up . . ."

He kissed me on the neck and shoulders as I continued to prattle on about scrunchies and ponytails. When he got to my mouth, I finally stopped stammering and kissed him back. After some stumbling around in the safe-sex department, we ended up making love. Not on the antique bed with down pillows and comforter, but on the floor of the spare room, surrounded by ribbons of paper towels and piles of T-shirts.

The only other guy I had been with was Peter. But that relationship seemed like preschool compared to the way things were evolving with Kip.

I spent the next hour drifting in and out of sleep, blanketed by Kip's words.

NOTES TO SELF:

● Next time with Kip—more of the same, thank you
very much.
● See if Kip's mom will decorate my room.
● Submit applications online or by mail—decide!
● If a cannibal ate a clown, would it taste funny?
Enough with the one-liners; I need a set that builds.
● The harvest dance was almost fun—I knew Kip
didn't really want to be there, but he was a good
sport. I'm glad we went, but I'm over it.

Every college application stressed the same thing: "Your personal statement is the most important factor in the admissions process." I weighed the various options. SERIOUS—list all my academic achievements and extracurricular activities. SERIOUS YET FUN—discuss my love of comedy and film, the diversity of my home and neighborhood. Or just REAL—Hey, you there, Admissions Officer! Things are *great*. My life used to be about as exciting as a glass of water sitting on a counter. Now it's suddenly a glass of tropical punch—tangy, colorful, full of fizz. In fact, Dear Sir/Madam, before Kip I never knew how much of the human experience I'd been missing out on. Therefore, the chances of me contributing to your university have increased exponentially. Dare I say it—? You'll be kicking yourself in the head for years if you don't scoop me up for your freshman class *now*. Hitch up your wagon to me, University of FILL IN THE BLANK, 'cause I am going places!

In the end, of course, I went with a semi-traditional statement—with a few humorous touches buried in the text. I procrastinated and sent in my online applications seconds before the November 30 deadline. (What was the hurry? So I could spend the next three or four months sitting by the mailbox?)

Abby applied to CalBerkeley, confident that the universe wanted her to stay in the Bay Area. Kip and I applied there too. Before we met, almost three months ago, neither of us thought we'd apply so close to home, but now a stay-together-in–San Francisco backup plan seemed like a good idea. Northwestern had been my first choice (because of its proximity to the famed Second City), but lately moving to Chicago seemed out of the question. UCLA was now the most serious contender. L.A. was less than an hour-and-a-half plane ride away, with lots of opportunities for honing my stand-up skills. Kip applied to some schools in L.A. too. Although his grades and test scores were lower than mine, his personal statement was so sharp and edgy, it could have been posted on the Internet.

⌁

Mr. Perez finally let me run the full-day *Vertigo* tour. We started in the city, visiting the sights of the 1958 Hitchcock classic, which included Mission Dolores, Fort Point, and Scottie's apartment on Lombard Street. The crowd ate them up. Because we went south to Big Basin Redwoods State Park and San Juan Bautista, this was *the* tour for the film's many die-hard fans; our once-a-month buses were always full.

Vertigo was one of my favorite movies of all time, but compared to the rabid fans who took our tour, I came off as a novice.

"This is the location of Madeleine's apartment at the Empire Hotel." I explained that they only shot the exteriors here, that Hitchcock used a soundstage on the Paramount lot to shoot the interiors. The Hitchcock fans snapped photos of the faded brownstone tucked into the now-trendy Nob Hill neighborhood.

The bus was so jammed—Mr. Perez notoriously overbooked whenever he could—that I could barely see someone raising his hand in the back. I walked toward the guy with the hat and skateboard in his lap. I had to put down the microphone so the crowd wouldn't hear me laugh when I realized it was Kip.

"Don't you think Judy should've sensed there was trouble in the relationship?" he asked. "I mean, Scottie doesn't love her for who she is, but for who he wants her to be."

Okay, keep it together. "There's a lot of denial going on, that's for sure," I said.

A slow smile spread across his face. "Sexual tension too."

I walked back to the front of the bus before my laughter got me fired.

I took the seat behind Mr. Perez as he drove down Route 101 toward San Juan Bautista. As the tourists disembarked for lunch, I pulled Kip aside and told him he was out of his mind.

"What are you talking about? This is great!" he said.

"I never knew you were such a fan."

"I had to watch it again last night to bone up. Talk about material—these people are insane."

When he removed his baseball hat, his long dark curls blew in the breeze. He then reached into his pack and took out a small blanket, which he held down on the grass with his sneakers. I grabbed two box lunches from the cooler; Kip grinned when I couldn't open the resealable wrap on my sandwich.

On the way back from throwing out our trash, Kip dove to catch a wayward Frisbee for a group of kids. He tossed it back with a wave while several girls our age checked him out from another blanket. Barefoot, in his hospital pants and They Might Be Giants T-shirt, he was oblivious to how good-looking he was. I gazed up at the Mission—minus the special-effects bell tower they used in the movie—and wondered what I'd done to deserve someone like him.

Whatever it was, *that* should have been on my personal statement.

One of the best things about San Francisco is the weather, especially in the early winter. While people in other parts of the country are shoveling driveways and scraping windshields, we're walking around in windbreakers, basking in the sun. Here, the winters are crisp and amazing.

Of course, being in love didn't hurt either.

I listened attentively to my mother's "chats" about curfews, moderation, and trust.

Whatever you say, Mom.

Then I snuck out to see Kip anyway.

He and I spent every possible minute together, which, given my senior-year schedule, was nowhere near enough. I showed up for as many of my yearbook meetings as possible without getting kicked off the committee. Running the debate club was actually something I enjoyed. (My ulterior motive—more time onstage.) Abby disagreed with my strategy for getting into a good school. Her theory was to bag the extracurriculars and concentrate on a killer essay backed up with a few audition tapes as insurance. She figured she was a great candidate for any school, and the last thing she intended to do was have a stressed-out senior year.

Kip was another one enjoying life to the fullest. He got a mention in *The Guardian* for his set at the Punch Line, and his job at the frame shop was a no-brainer. One afternoon, I arrived home to find him and Christopher in the living room, both wearing their underwear outside their pants and towels around their necks as capes. They raced through the house like Captain Underpants while Delilah and I cheered them on. (Hands off, Lois Lane; the superhero in the polka-dot boxers is mine.)

After that, we explored the library upstairs, a room I was embarrassed to admit I hardly ever used.

"Are you kidding?!" Kip asked. "This is a gold mine!"

We sat on the floor and made notes—me in my journal, Kip on his paper towels—about anything even remotely funny. Creative visualization? The history of the Oscars? *National Geographic*? The room seemed brimming with possibilities.

In fact, when we were together, it was as if time slowed down and every gum wrapper on the sidewalk, every cloud in the sky, was imbued with meaning. The universe *spoke* to me as it never had done before. If some scientist had bumped into me on the street and asked me to help him find the cure for cancer, I *could* have, that's how plugged in to the inner workings of the world I felt. My physics homework made sense—of course those atoms formed a chain! Even Christopher's Legos snapped magically into labyrinthine designs. My mind exploded with thoughts and ideas; I jotted down notes every few moments, an avalanche of material that would last me for months—if I only got around to joining the rest of the world and working again.

As Abby was quick to remind me.

"Look, I'm happy you have a boyfriend—I am! But you missed two gigs and an audition last week."

"I heard the crowd was so bad you couldn't buy a laugh with a fistful of fifties."

Abby didn't take my detour. "You're turning into one of those girls we hate!" she continued. "A girl like Lynda, who only joins the living between boyfriends."

"Don't even say that! I had two yearbook meetings and three tests—I'm swamped." I didn't tell her a huge chunk of my time had been spent just talking to Kip on the phone when I wasn't with him. If she had known I'd had to change the billing plan on my cell phone twice in the past three months, it would only have added fuel to the fire.

"I just *miss* you," Abby said. "I never see you anymore."

"*I* miss me," I said. "I've been getting up at six to study, I'm doing homework during dinner. It's ridiculous."

She softened a bit. "I want to give you your Christmas present."

"How about Tuesday? No, no—Wednesday, around eight?"

"Whenever you can squeeze me in," Abby said.

It was my turn to soften. "You going to open-mike tomorrow?"

Her face finally brightened. "Wait till you hear my new set. A whole Barbie thing. Melanoma Barbie, Bi-polar Barbie, Bulimic Barbie . . . Listen to this—if Barbie is so popular, why do you have to buy her friends?"

I was almost envious, not only of Abby's new set but of the time she had to work on it, even *with* her new boyfriend, Jacob. I was determined to finish the set-ups I'd written with Kip in our library. I knew I had to get out to the clubs more often; I didn't want my comedy skills to get flabby while the rest of me reveled in Planet Kip.

—————

After school, I met Kip at the frame shop, then we headed down to Fisherman's Wharf. As we approached a small hair salon, he looked at his watch. "Right on time." He grabbed a chair in the waiting room and picked up a magazine.

I asked him what we were doing there.

"It's your last Christmas present," he said.

He had already made me five cd's with the songs he continually sang when we were together. I'd gotten him several great shirts from Goodwill. (His favorite was a blue work shirt from Tom's Garage with MECHANIC embroidered over the breast pocket. He had worn it at the Comedy Stop the week before and looked great.)

I grabbed my huge hunk of hair. "Getting my hair cut is *not* my idea of a present."

"Are you kidding? No one takes scissors to that mane of yours as long as I'm around." When he bent down to tie his hiking boots, a photo of the two of us fell out of his shirt pocket. He picked it up and blushed.

A few minutes later, a whippet-thin woman named Marla called Kip's name.

"We're on," he said.

I began to get nervous when he sat me down in Marla's chair.

"My girlfriend, Becky, needs some help."

"You have great hair," Marla told me.

"So I thought you could give us some lessons," Kip said.

"You want me to show her how to style her hair?"

"No, I want you to show *me* how to style her hair."

"Well, aren't you Mr. Right?"

She winked at me, and I smiled back.

Marla began by separating my tumble into three sections, then showed Kip how to weave from left to right.

When she finished, she undid the braid and he tried. Fifteen painstaking minutes later, he was finished.

Marla held up the hand mirror so I could see the back. I had to admit, it looked amazing.

"Funny with great hair," Kip said. "You could be Julia Louis-Dreyfus."

"Minus the *Seinfeld* royalties."

Marla then showed Kip how to twist my hair up, even fasten it with chopsticks. To be honest, having Kip styling my hair seemed bizarre, but I found the effort and thought endearing.

Kip paid the receptionist, and we headed back toward my house.

I stammered a thank-you. "No one's ever taken such a personal interest in me before," I said.

"I can't understand why." He turned to face me. "God, you're gorgeous."

My soul ate up the compliment like a hungry child scoffing bread. My clothes usually left marks on my slightly padded body, my contact lens case was gunked with solution, I couldn't go anywhere without a wad of tissues in my pocket during pollen season. On most days, I felt like I was waiting for the world to discover what a semi-mess I was. But seen through Kip's eyes, I was something else entirely.

A person could get used to this.

At dinner, Mom gushed over my hair—"It's finally off your face!"—to say nothing of Delilah, who insisted on trying out my chopsticks.

I lay in bed that night shell-shocked from all the attention.

Until the shock went from inside my head to out, shaking the house, rattling the windows.

"Don't panic!" my father called from the next room.

It was two-fifteen in the morning. For some reason, every earthquake I'd ever experienced had taken place at night. This one felt like the house was riding to shore on a wave.

My mother ran into my room holding a half-asleep Christopher. Dad followed.

The four of us sat in my room and listened to everything we own shake. Like most people in the Bay Area, we made sure the shelves and bookcases were fastened to the walls, with nothing—not even pictures—hanging over the beds.

After a few seconds, the tremor stopped.

"A five or a six," my father said.

"No way," Mom replied. "At least a seven."

"Seven or eight," I added.

Like judges holding up cards, we guessed how this one

would register on the Richter scale. Mom took Christopher back to bed.

Dad shut off the light and asked if I was okay.

"Shaken, not stirred."

He turned the light back on. "I just want you to be safe," he said. "That's all."

"God, Dad! I'm fine."

He stood in the doorway, looking so helpless I wondered who was supposed to take care of whom.

He turned off the light again. "Night, sweetie."

I knew I wouldn't be able to fall back to sleep, so I got online. As soon as I logged on, Kip IM'ed me. How did people ever have relationships before instant messaging?

"You all right?" he asked.

I wrote back that I was.

"I can't imagine anything happening to you," he wrote.

"Nothing's going to happen," I responded.

"In that case, what do you think of this routine?"

We worked on his jokes for half an hour before we signed off. I had given him a few good suggestions; it made me eager to work on my own material. I laughed in anticipation of what I knew Abby would say about the earthquake tomorrow: "Hey, it's not San Andrea's fault!" The joke never got a laugh in the clubs, but she loved it and used it all the time anyway.

The next morning, I jumped when I came downstairs—Kip was sitting at the kitchen table having coffee with my mother.

"They say it was a 6.2," he said. "Biggest one in a while."

I asked him what he was doing here.

"Figured I'd test out my new skills." He pointed to the kitchen stool and told me to sit.

Delilah stood next to him and observed him at work on my hair, throwing in a few pointers of her own. Before long, I had a beautiful braid halfway down my back.

My mother brought our cups to the sink. "Reminds me of braiding your hair in grade school. Maybe I should start packing your lunch again too."

I was going out with someone who put 200 percent into the relationship, who loved me more than anyone else ever had.

Couldn't she just let me be happy?

NOTES TO SELF:

● Absolutely, by far, the best Christmas ever. Such
an original gift from Kip. Now, if my mom would
just shut up about how weird it was that he came
over to braid my hair. Get over it, okay?
● New Year's Eve—pretending to be at Abby's—a
great night.
● Kip freaked when Charlie—stoner lab partner
from hell—played with my braid outside school.
"Who is he? Why did he touch your hair? Does he
have a girlfriend?" I mean, it's Charlie, for
chrissakes. From now on, don't mention him to Kip in
conversation. (None of Abby's boyfriends were ever
this jealous. Kip and I must be on a whole different
level.)

From the Paper Towel Dialogues of
Kip Costello

Happy New Year! I hope this one's better than last year. Can we turn the page on being the new guy in school? Hey—I go here now, okay?

I felt like an imbecile taking Becky to the hairdresser's—thank God, no one from school saw me. But Becky complains about her hair all the time—I thought she'd really appreciate it. I think she did.

Don't know why that guy Charlie was teasing her, though. Sure, do your labs together, but that's it, okay? Get your own girlfriend and keep your hands to yourself.

I hope next semester isn't so busy for Becky. It's not like we need to be together 24/7, but I'd be happy if she was a little more available.

Those earthquakes still scare the hell out of me. You have no control, no power over any of it. I <u>hate</u> that.

A woman Abby's size dropped off a box of vintage dresses at the Goodwill during my shift. I priced and paid for them before anyone else in the store even got to take a look. I knew I wouldn't be able to wait till Abby's birthday and would end up handing over my score later in the day.

After my shift ended, I headed to Safeway to meet Abby. When she first got the job stocking shelves, I thought for sure it was to gather material for her act. But no, she really enjoyed lining up the boxes of detergent, the cans of corn. She called the whole process very Zen. Of course, that didn't stop her from constantly putting products in the wrong places or covering up the bar codes with happy-face stickers. She had such an uncanny knack for never getting caught, she had actually been promoted to assistant manager two months earlier.

Abby shrieked down the aisle when I handed her the dresses. I knew the blue beaded one would knock her out, and it did.

"I could get old-fashioned glasses and do a whole retro set," she said.

Only someone as beautiful as Abby could purposefully try to make herself look wacky and unattractive and still come off gorgeous.

She punched out, and we headed downtown to the library to work on our Lit projects. We settled at a table in the corner of the periodicals room.

"I can't just start right in," Abby said. "I need to get the creative juices flowing."

"Not the cd's again."

"They're crying out to me."

"They check them at the front desk."

"Not on a busy Saturday with that old lady working."

Abby headed to the audiovisual department to play her usual game of removing cd's from one box and switching them to another. I covered her back.

"I'm performing a service," she said. "Some poor dope who takes out *Oklahoma!* gets turned on to Miles Davis instead. He should *thank* me."

She asked if I wanted to go with her to visit Jacob when we finished. I told her I was headed to Kip's.

"Surprise, surprise."

"I haven't seen him since Thursday."

"Wow, two whole days."

I'd had enough of her unsolicited comments. "This

isn't some stupid crush." I waited till I had her undivided attention. "I love him. A lot."

"It's been nice talking with you, but I have to scream now."

I ignored her and continued. My mind suddenly couldn't remember where the brakes were because I kept going. About how I never thought I could love anyone like this. About how much Kip and I were perfect for each other.

"This isn't just *love*," I said. "This . . . this is something different."

Abby looked at me, dumbfounded. "Are you saying that your love is 'special'? Better than the run-of-the-mill love that *other* people have? Because that would be the sickest, most narcissistic thing I've ever heard."

"Look, I'm sorry you don't get it."

"I'm just trying to understand how a guy who keeps you chained to your cell phone like it's one of those prison bracelets can possibly hold the patent on a new kind of love."

I told her to calm down, that other people could hear her. She didn't care.

"And if you use the word soulmate one more time, I'm going to lose it."

Why couldn't I share these feelings with her? Why couldn't she be my best friend and just *listen*?

There was so much more I wanted to tell her: How Kip had blurted out "I love you" in the popcorn line at the movies—the very first time anyone outside my family had directed those incredibly important words my way. How embarrassed we both were by the spontaneity of the phrase that night, but how the words were now broken-in and comfortable, like a favorite woolen sweater. I could've shared so much with Abby if she'd been willing to open her mind and hear me. Kip had been telling me that love as intense as ours scared most people away, and I was beginning to think he was right. Abby and I went back to our table and worked on our projects in silence.

Because Abby's boyfriend worked near Kip's apartment, she and I headed to Noe Valley together even though we'd barely spoken all afternoon.

"Look, I'm sorry about before," she finally said. "I'm happy for you, I really am. But the whole our-love-is-different thing sounds like you think your relationship is better than other people's, and that's just wrong."

"I never said we're better—that's ridiculous."

"Whatever," Abby said. "I just want you to be happy."

"I am."

"I'm glad." We both smiled, ignoring the tension that still filled the air.

When we got to Kip's apartment, I told Abby I'd see her on Monday.

"Can I come up and use the bathroom? The one at Jacob's store is disgusting."

It made perfect sense. Abby needed a bathroom, and Kip's apartment was right here. So why did I think Kip would mind?

"There's a Burger King on the corner," I said. "It might be faster."

It was as if I had hit Abby in the head with a brick. "You want me to use the bathroom at the *Burger King*? I'll go to the 7-Eleven and buy a box of Depends before I do that." She dug her heels in even deeper. "What am I going to find in Kip's apartment—him dancing around in your underwear?"

"Don't be stupid. It's just . . ."

She waited for me to continue. Unfortunately I had nothing to say that made any sense. She looked so disappointed, but the crazy part was, I could understand why. I was the one acting like an idiot. I told her to come up.

As I climbed the stairs to his apartment, I hoped Kip wouldn't be weird about the surprise. But why was I so worried? Was our relationship so hermetically sealed that a three-way conversation was impossible?

We could hear him singing from outside the apartment. I knocked, and he answered the door with a "Hey, Beck." His face changed when he saw Abby.

"Abby needs to use the bathroom," I said.

"I'm ready to burst," she added.

We looked at Kip expectantly.

"Yeah, sure." He smiled. "Come on in." He showed Abby to the bathroom, then returned to the kitchen.

"Is she hanging out with us all night?" he asked quietly.

I told Kip she was meeting Jacob a few blocks away. He looked relieved.

"I mean, we can do something with them if you want," he said. "I was thinking we'd be alone, but if—"

"No, no. She's just using the bathroom." I smiled as if everything were fine. I hoped it was.

When Abby emerged, I knew exactly what she'd do—gush over the apartment, checking out each piece.

"You're so lucky!" she told Kip. "This place is unbelievable!" She sat on the barber chair in the kitchen. She pulled the lever, making the chair go up and down. The expression on her face was so full of joy, I wished I had my camera.

"Beck, you said this place was amazing, but I had no idea—"

Kip coughed.

Abby got the hint and climbed out of the chair. "No problem. You two probably have plans."

We both nodded.

"Well, if you're looking for something to do later, Jacob and I will be at the Depot."

"I hear the Depot is great." The second the words left my mouth, I was sorry.

"Cheap too. You'd like it." She shrugged, then looked at Kip.

The conversation descended into a silence large enough to fill a black hole.

"We haven't decided what we're doing," I finally said. "Maybe we'll meet you later."

"Should I save you a table?"

She was pushing now, trying to prove a point.

"That's okay—we'll take our chances," Kip said.

Abby took another look around the room before heading out the door. We listened to her footsteps on the stairs until she was gone.

"Is it me, or was that totally weird?" Kip asked.

I told him Abby loved to play with people's minds.

I spent the next twenty minutes goofing on my old best friend with my new best friend. Kip imitated Abby checking out the room; I made fun of her telling the same stories at dinner I'd heard a hundred times before. I didn't care how anti-social Abby thought Kip and I were.

There was no place else either of us wanted to be.

NOTES TO SELF:

● Think of a backup plan in case every school I applied to rejects me.

● Bring my brown pants to Goodwill next time I work—Kip's right, I do look a little fat in them.

● I could've worked in those two women in the front row last night. Don't be so afraid to trust the audience.

● Don't mention Abby so much to Kip—I think she bugs him. And Jacob—I kind of agree with Kip, he does seem like a snob.

From the Paper Towel Dialogues of
Kip Costello

Spent the day outside, writing six fresh squares of jokes—is there anything better than sitting in the afternoon sun, putting down words with your favorite pen? I don't think so.

Seeing Becky later—not to be sappy, but it's our four-month anniversary. Made her some more cd's. She loved "Wichi Tai To" when she heard it here. She'll go crazy.

I was disappointed when she couldn't come to the skateboard tournament last Saturday. I would've done much better if she'd been there. I felt bad the whole thing turned into a fight, but in the end, she agreed with me that we needed to keep the focus on each other. I mean, I'd drop anything for her—it should be vice versa, right?

I've been itching to hit the road again. I'm getting sick of the same old clubs. I'd like to check out the coast, maybe all the way to L.A. or San Diego—with Becky, of course. (Probably have to wait till she's out of the house for that one.) The clubs, the museums, the boardwalk—so many places I want to show her.

Here's my worst fear for a college roommate—she's wearing a PETA T-shirt, talking about how cockroaches are human too. . . .

Every time I visited a prospective college, I pretended I was going there for a gig. I pictured flyers around the campus advertising my show, imagined myself standing on the auditorium stage, delivering razor-sharp material to thunderous applause. (The reality was nowhere near as interesting, of course—meeting in front of the admissions office with a group of other kids and parents, waiting for the volunteer student guide to begin the memorized tour.)

UCLA was the only school I'd applied to that my parents and I didn't visit last fall. So Mom bought two tickets in late January for the two of us to fly to L.A. It would still be another two months before I heard from my prospective schools.

The eager-beaver junior who ran the tour might as well have been shaking pom-poms for all his cheeriness. He showed us the obligatory classrooms, labs, and sample dorm. The room looked like every other dorm room we'd seen in the past few months—more prison cell than home-away-from-home. I checked out the two twin beds on either side of the tiny room and couldn't imagine the logistics of Kip visiting for the weekend.

At the health services building, our guide pointed out a large bulletin board listing various support group meetings. "Whatever you need, we've got it," he said.

I glanced at my watch and hoped we'd be breaking for lunch soon.

In the cafeteria, I checked the five messages waiting on my cell phone.

"How's it going?" Kip asked when I called him back.

I told him that at this point all the schools I'd looked at were merging into one institutional blur.

"I'm going to fight so hard to keep you in the Bay Area, I'll be getting calls from Washington offering me lobbyist positions."

I looked over at my mother waiting in the rental car semi-patiently.

"I got my laptop back today," he said. "So you can pick yours up when you get back on Tuesday."

Which to my mind was not soon enough. I told him I loved him, then joined my mother at the car.

"If we eat before five-thirty, we can take advantage of the early-bird special," she said.

"You know I have to turn this into a routine," I told her.

"Millionaire mom who makes us eat dinner at lunchtime to save seven dollars."

"It's yours."

We ate at a small Mexican restaurant near the hotel, then hightailed it back to our room to watch the pay-per-view.

I just wanted to get home.

I was about to change into my pajamas when Mom handed me my jacket. I asked her where we were going; she told me it was a surprise.

"What? If we eat breakfast now, it's half-price?"

"Very funny," she said. "No, I thought we might stop by the Comedy Store."

Now she had my attention. "Are you kidding?"

"If it's open-mike night, you can put your name in."

I ran to the bathroom, put on mascara, and fixed my hair, just in case. The Comedy Store was an institution; surely there would be a long list of hopefuls on any given night. The chances were slim I'd get called. But even to be in the audience would be a treat.

"I thought you'd be dying to check out the local clubs," she said. "I'm surprised you didn't ask."

"I knew you'd be tired after walking around campus all day. I didn't want to push it." I didn't mention the reason I hadn't brought it up was that Kip had made me promise not to explore the clubs without him.

On the way down to the lobby, I veered away from my mother and called Kip.

"You promised!" he yelled. "We were going to do it together!"

"Well, my mom surprised me—what am I going to say, no?"

"If you really loved me, you would."

"Excuse me?"

He sounded about ten years old. I told him we probably wouldn't even be able to get in.

"Are you going to try and *perform*?"

I glanced at the tape recorder and notebook peeking out of my bag. "No, of course not."

By the lobby door, my mother looked as if her patience was wearing thin. I told Kip I'd call him after the show.

My mother jingled the car keys in her hands. "Did Kip ask if you brushed your teeth too?"

"It's not any different than Dad packing you that food to take on the plane," I said. "Is it so weird that someone cares about me?"

She actually looked hurt. "Of course it's not weird someone cares about you. You *deserve* to be cared about. It just seems a little much sometimes, that's all."

I looked her in the eye, dead-on. "We love each other. It's that simple."

This time she looked as if she was hiding a smile. "It's never that simple," she said. "Being in a relationship is the most complicated thing in the world."

As we drove to the Comedy Store, I clenched and unclenched my fists, trying to work out my nerves. If I actually got to perform, it would be the highlight of my comedy résumé, hands down.

But the bouncer stopped us dead in our tracks. "Tonight's bringer night," he said.

Figures. I headed back toward the car.

"What's bringer night?" my mother asked.

"Rick doesn't believe in them, so I've never had to do it. It means you bring eight people in with you if you want to perform—eight people who'll pay the ten bucks cover, eight people who'll pay the two-drink minimum."

"Sounds like blackmail," Mom said. "Taking advantage of people who want to get onstage."

"That about sums it up. Come on."

My mother didn't budge. Instead, she went back to cross-examine the poor bouncer. "How about this?" she asked. "I'll pay for eight people, even though it's only the two of us."

"Lady, it's a Monday night. We're trying to fill seats. You need eight bodies." He went back inside.

"We'll just have to find another way," she said.

"I appreciate the effort. Paying *extra*—that's big for you."

Her face suddenly brightened. "Here's where we have a chance to spend that money we saved with our early-bird dinner."

We walked down Sunset Boulevard until we noticed a couple of old guys hanging out in front of a liquor store. They looked like they were recuperating from a weeklong bender.

"Mom, no."

"Don't be judgmental. I bet they'd love to help us out."

"Especially with the two-drink minimum."

I have never loved my mother more than when I was watching her pitch a free night in the "real L.A." to everyone who walked by. When we headed back to the club with our six new friends, I gave my name to the manager.

I tried to call Kip, but the line was busy; I called Abby instead.

She went crazy. "The Comedy Store! You're my hero!"

I told her I had a fifty-fifty chance of performing and would call her later.

I joined my mother in the back of the club. Our new

friends had pushed together a few small tables and ordered their first drinks.

The manager gave me the high sign from across the bar. I was in.

One of the guys from the liquor store stood up and applauded. "We're with you, Becky! With you all the way."

I bent down near my mother's chair. "Don't let anyone get too carried away."

"Well, I guess that just depends on how funny you are."

The manager brought me backstage to prepare. A guy named Mike Leone introduced himself; he was a senior at Burbank High, performing here for the third time. He was wiry, talked fast, and had more cowlicks than I'd ever seen on one head. It was comforting to have someone my own age to wait with.

The manager motioned for Mike, then told me I was next. I jumped up and down, prepped my tape recorder, took some deep breaths. I went to the ladies' room, tried to make sense out of my hair. The index cards peeked out from my bag—BE HERE NOW. ARE YOU HERE OR SOMEWHERE ELSE?

I was *here*, at the Comedy Store, earning my first fee for performing. It was only fifty dollars—it didn't even dent how much Mom had spent, especially when you added in all the drinks—but for me, it marked the difference between amateur and semi-professional.

I watched the end of Mike's energetic set—a high-tech surfer dude in Silicon Valley—and was impressed. When he left the stage, I congratulated him.

He pointed to my bag. "You want me to watch that?"

In my haste, I had forgotten that Abby wouldn't be here with me for our usual bag-watching. I handed it to him as the manager introduced me.

"Ladies and gentlemen—all the way from San Francisco—Becky Martin."

I did my getting-your-license set—the elderly driving instructor with a bladder the size of a raisin who made me pull over every two blocks so he could pee; the marching-band music he insisted on playing that made me feel as if we were driving in a surreal parade. I got a few laughs on the joke about studying for the photo test, but it still needed work. When I did the bit about how stupid it was to need a driver's license to buy beer when you can't drink and drive, one woman in the front row actually yelped.

All in all, a solid set. Our table in the back applauded like crazy.

"I owe you one," I told my mother back at my seat. "Big time."

Mike made his way to our table with my bag.

"You were so relaxed up there," he said. "Really good."

I told him I loved his bit about the microchip in the surfboard.

Mike suggested moving even more tables together and having his family and friends join us. Before long, we took up the entire back of the room, cheering the comics on the back end of the bill. I scanned our group, a hodgepodge of people with nothing in common but laughter. When Mike's uncle Jack took a photo, he had to use the wide angle to get us all in.

"Would you mind sending me a copy?" my mom asked Mike. "This really is a night to remember."

She gave him our address and e-mails. Outside on the sidewalk, the sixteen of us hugged good-bye like old friends. Mike said he'd call if he ever made it up to San Francisco.

When I got Kip on the phone, the words burst from me like an avalanche, describing every detail of the night.

"You got *on*?"

"Aren't you happy for me?" I asked. "I finally got paid!"

"Of course, I'm happy. I just wish I was there too."

"That makes two of us."

"You let some guy you didn't know hold your stuff? Suppose he went through your wallet and wrote down your address or your credit card number?"

"He *has* my address. He's sending us the group picture."

"You gave some strange guy your address? Are you nuts?"

"My mother gave it to him!"

Silence. "So your mother likes this guy. . . ."

Why was Kip getting this upset? "He was just some guy. He was nobody." Maybe if I switched the subject. "My mom was amazing. And Abby was more excited than I was."

"You already talked to Abby? Jeez, am I the last person to find out anything around here?"

My mother started the car; I told Kip I'd call him tomorrow. But he called me back several times. When we returned to the hotel, I closed the bathroom door and sat on the edge of the tub to continue our conversation.

"I can't believe you had one of the best nights of your life and I wasn't there."

"It would have been a much better night if you were here, believe me."

"This guy Mike—I don't have to worry about him, right?"

"You have nothing to worry about. I assure you." Of

course, *I* had something to worry about—my mother now stood in the bathroom doorway.

"Hang up that phone right now and shut the power off. That's enough for one day."

I waited for her to leave before I hung up.

I climbed into my bed expecting the inevitable. She didn't let me down.

"You are too young to be so involved with one person. He is suffocating you."

"No he's not."

"You better take it down a few notches, Beck. I mean it."

I shut off the light without answering her.

Mom obviously didn't understand. For her, this was all about keeping me under wraps, not wanting her little girl to leave the nest. I was eighteen next month; how long did she think she could control me? I made a mental note to keep my phone off when I was with her, talk to Kip from school or in my room, speak about him less. I just had to work around her.

~

Back in San Francisco the next afternoon, I asked my mother to drop me at Kip's so I could get my laptop. She said she would wait for me in the car.

"Just drop me off. I'll be home in an hour," I pleaded.

"Sorry, honey. You've got ten minutes."

I slammed the door and ran up the stairs two at a time. Kip would be furious when he found out I couldn't stay.

He pulled me into the apartment and kissed me non-stop. This was the longest we'd been apart, and I couldn't get enough of him. We knocked the vase with the bamboo stalks all over the floor, then ended up on top of them like two rain-forest animals.

I hated to interrupt him with the news. "My mother's downstairs."

"What?"

I got up and smoothed myself off.

"You're kidding me, right?" he said.

"Unfortunately not."

He picked up a piece of bamboo and tickled my chin. "But I missed you."

"I missed you too. Desperately."

"There's so much to talk about." He continued to tickle me with the bamboo. "Like how often you visit the Phish fan sites. Or the IMDb."

I pulled away from him and laughed. "Did you open my History file? Even my mom's never checked the Web sites I go to."

"And all those chatty e-mails . . ."

I stopped laughing. "You read my *e-mails*?"

"Wouldn't you read mine if you had *my* computer?"

I asked him how he got my password.

"Oh, like you haven't checked your e-mail here enough times. But why didn't you mention us when people asked what was new?"

The bamboo began to annoy me. I pushed it away from my face. "What are you talking about?"

"When Harley5 asked what was new, you talked about school."

"That's my old English teacher who moved to Hartford. Why would I tell her about us?"

"Oh, like I'm not important?"

"Of course you are."

"Did you tell that guy in L.A. about us?"

"We were too busy watching everyone's sets! Why are you acting like this?"

"First, you break your promise about going to clubs without me, then you give your address to some guy. . . ."

Five minutes ago, we were great. How did things turn around so quickly?

Kip handed me my laptop and told me he'd call me later. I felt like a kid in grammar school being punished by the principal.

"So you're not coming over?" I asked.

He didn't look at me. "I don't think so."

He led me out of the apartment and shut the door.

I knocked several times. "Kip! What's wrong? What'd I do?"

He didn't answer. When I heard a car honk outside, I

knew it was my mother. "Kip!" One more knock. Two, three.

"Kip!" My knuckles ached.

At the next honk, I headed back downstairs. With each stair, I willed myself not to cry.

"All set?" my mom asked.

"Yeah."

She pulled into the traffic. "Your father said Christopher discovered the encyclopedia. Spent the whole night talking about aardvarks and aquaducts. We're all in trouble now."

I smiled even though my insides were collapsing. All evening, I pretended to listen while my mother talked about the campus, the comedy club, the nice people we had met. Blah, blah, blah. Later, I spent the night listening for the phone. It didn't ring. Whenever I called Kip, I got the machine. It took five phone calls and six e-mails before I began to feel desperate and pathetic. (Which in itself is desperate and pathetic.)

The next day, school was a fog. I hit the redial button so often on my cell, I practically wore the letters off. When Kip finally called late that afternoon, the wave of relief was so physical, I felt as if I had just thrown down a thousand-pound barbell.

"Are we okay?" I asked.

"I don't know, are we?"

I thought about how much I loved him, how I couldn't imagine not having him in my life.

"We're fine," I said.

"Good."

We made plans to meet later.

I stared at the ceiling of my room. Kip was sensitive; even the littlest things meant so much to him. I'd have to be more considerate, think of what the effects might be before I spoke. The relationship was such a good one, it was worth the work.

NOTES TO SELF:

● "I put in a lot of time studying for the part of my license that matters most—the photo. I mean, that little sucker follows you around for years, right? So the day of the shoot, I am prepared— three changes of wardrobe, plus props, makeup, bottled water. I'm expecting a guy with three assistants to be framing his hands around my face, telling me to make love to the camera. Instead I get a bifocaled bureaucrat with cream cheese on his tie telling me to stand behind the white line. Is it too much to ask for a little glamour at the DMV?" Nailed it—finally.

● Take the photo Mike sent off the fridge. Why ask for trouble with Kip?

● Tell Abby to stop making a big deal about my debut at the Comedy Store. Kip feels bad enough.

● Be careful with e-mails in case Kip gets the bright idea of checking them remotely. I should hide this notebook too.

● I'm almost 18—bring it on.

From the Paper Towel Dialogues of
Kip Costello

I kind of feel bad about all the grief I've been giving Becky lately. Between her new jeans, that trip to L.A., and reading those e-mails—her face just kind of collapsed in disappointment each time. Maybe I shouldn't be so hard on her. . . . No, no—I have to be.

I mean, what happens if she bops up and down the coast in her tight new jeans and finds someone better? <u>Then</u> what do I do? I hate feeling this needy—such a wuss. I like having a girlfriend, but I don't like how it makes me feel half the time. I hate keeping her on such a tight leash, but I have to know where I stand.

Mike e-mailed me several times over the next month, mostly to share news of upcoming auditions and shows between here and L.A. I deleted them as soon as I could, in case Kip got the urge to check my messages.

But even with the more frequent comments about my appearance or my friends, my relationship with Kip seemed as necessary to me as flossing. I checked in with him several times a day and couldn't imagine not running the minute details of my life by him. His advice was always well thought-out, but most important, he didn't feel burdened by the litany of my daily events. In fact, he got annoyed if I *didn't* tell him everything.

Kip had four gigs up north that he'd scheduled before we met. Because it was the weekend of my birthday, he suggested I accompany him up to Mendocino. His theory was that I was now eighteen and my mother couldn't stop me.

Boy, was he wrong.

Kip's reaction to my mother's emphatic NO was typical of his growing annoyance with my friends and family. "Why did you ask her? You should have just *told* her," he said. "She doesn't care about you as much as I do—*I'm* the one looking out for you."

But a small part of me didn't mind being forced to stay in the city without him—the part of me that desperately missed my best friend.

Abby slept over for the weekend, bringing a full itinerary. First off, we threw Christopher a bone. Since he could never come to the clubs, he always begged us to put on special shows for him. We relented, letting him emcee our sets in the family room. He even lassoed Delilah into singing. Her version of "Hollywood Swinging" was one for the books.

For my birthday, Abby treated me to dinner at the Indian restaurant near the Zen Center. We ate saag paneer and reminisced about some of our (her) old pranks. My favorite: when Abby pretended to lose a contact (she doesn't wear them) during freshman assembly. The two of us had three rows of teachers and students crawling around the floor for fifteen minutes while we both yelled, "Careful not to step on it!"

We made so much noise yakking over dinner that the people at the next table actually moved.

Back at my house, Abby handed me a box wrapped with the Sunday comics.

Inside was a bean-bag frog.

"This is *so* not funny," I said. "Besides, this isn't a Leap Year. I'm only four and a half."

"I *thought* you and Christopher looked like twins." She handed me another smaller box.

I unwrapped the tissue paper and took out three strings of wooden beads.

"They're meditation beads. One hundred and eight on each strand. You count them off like a rosary."

"They're beautiful." I slipped them over my head. "If I just wear them and don't meditate, do I get bad karma or something?"

"Not any more than usual."

We spent the rest of the night listening to music and thinking up jokes for the voice balloons that threatened to overtake my movie-poster wall. The next morning we did Zen community service; I'd missed the last two weeks and was anxious to make up the time.

I was also behind in sending out audition tapes; luckily Abby was in need of some additional tapes too. It was nice to be back in the old routine: brainstorming in my basement, punching up jokes, and videotaping ourselves to weed out annoying mannerisms.

"After you take the mike off the stand, move it to the side so it's not sitting in the middle of the stage like a coatrack," Abby suggested.

I told her to stop saying "like" and "totally" so much during her set.

We taped ourselves in four different outfits, then Abby changed into some of the vintage dresses I had snagged from the thrift store.

We plugged the videocamera into the VCR to transfer the tapes to VHS. Neither Abby nor I was particularly technical by nature, especially me, but because of the many tapes we'd made over the years, we knew enough to get by. We watched ourselves a few times, laughing at our misses as much as our hits. We worked all afternoon and evening—editing, typing letters, addressing envelopes. We were ready.

I handed Abby the bowl of popcorn I'd scorched in the microwave. Idea for a set—how I didn't inherit Dad's gourmet gene.

"This is the best," Abby said.

"What are you talking about? It's barely edible."

"No, the popcorn is horrible, as usual. This"—she pointed to the two of us on the couch—"*this* is the best."

I had to agree with her; I missed us too.

"So, things are good, right? With Kip?"

"Really good."

"Great." She picked through the burnt kernels. "It's too bad you guys never do anything with Jacob and me. I gave up asking if you two want to get together."

What could I tell her—that Kip thought I didn't pay enough attention to him when Abby was around? That he found Jacob annoying? I felt bad enough when I realized

Jacob was in town this weekend; unlike me, Abby didn't need her boyfriend to be away to hang out with her best friend.

She put down the bowl of popcorn and stood on our makeshift stage. "Guess what we haven't done yet?"

I could feel the smile spread across my face. Best Friend Ritual #41—heckle practice. One of my favorites.

I tossed a handful of popcorn at her. "You *suck!*"

"Hey, buddy, newsflash—you're at a comedy club, not the movies."

"No kidding. I was expecting Julia Roberts and got you."

"I've heard Julia's stand-up; trust me, you're better off with me up here."

As usual, we started out tame and ended up using so many curse words Rick would have banned us from the club for a month.

I couldn't remember the last time Abby and I had laughed so hard.

Kip returned from the road at seven on Sunday; I was at his house by seven-ten.

He told me about crashing at his brother's friend's house and getting a standing ovation at his home club back in Napa. He said he couldn't wait to take me to

Mendocino. I told him about Abby and me making tapes to send out and showed him the beads she'd given me.

"Ahhh," he said. "But today's not really your birthday, is it, Ms. February Twenty-ninth?"

He jumped up from the bed, then handed me a box in the hand-painted wrapping paper I had admired at the frame store last time I was there. I pulled out the gilded nine-by-twelve frame and looked at the collage inside. It was a photo of me onstage at Rick's, one of my promo shots. But instead of the usually half-empty audience, the seats were filled with pictures of comedy's heaviest hitters. Dave Attell, Janeane Garofalo, Chris Rock, Whoopi Goldberg, and Jim Carrey sat in the audience laughing and applauding while I performed. The image was something I never would have come up with in even the most ambitious of dreams.

"Where did you get these photos?"

"Magazines, the Internet, all over." He pointed to the corner of the frame. "I especially like the heavenly section."

"Lenny Bruce, Sam Kinison, Phil Hartman . . . How long did this take you to do?"

He shrugged.

I squeezed his hand. "I don't think anyone's ever made me a present except for the painted macaroni necklaces Christopher used to do in preschool."

"Well, maybe this will bring you good luck with your new routines."

"I'll take all the help I can get."

"As long as you don't go with that chocoholic bit, you'll be fine."

I told him I had worked on it all weekend, that it was much funnier now.

He looked at me with disapproval. "You didn't put that on the tape, did you?"

I knew I should've run the tapes by Kip before I'd stuffed and addressed them to every club within a three-hundred-mile radius. But Abby and I had gone through the pain-in-the-butt ritual so many times before, it seemed silly to change the drill.

"Don't worry," I said. "It came out great."

He shook his head in disbelief. "I leave for three days, and you and Abby turn into two mad scientists trying to take over the comedy world."

"No, I—"

"I thought *I* was helping you."

"You are—I totally count on your input."

"I guess not anymore."

He took the collage from the bed and placed it back in its box. "Did you take my suggestions about the driving instructor jokes?"

"Yes, definitely. They were great."

Another disaster averted. I was getting better at zigzagging through the land mines of our conversations.

"Did you use the bit about putting plastic on the seats because the guy is so old you're afraid he's going to piss himself in your car?"

I told him that was the only one I didn't use.

"Why? You could work that one for more than a minute."

"It's just not me."

"What? Too gross? You need to push the envelope, Becky. I tell you that all the time."

I was drained from defending myself yet again. I picked up my purse from the floor and told him I had to go.

"You just got here!"

"I know, but I've got two tests tomorrow."

He looked at me in disbelief. "Didn't you study this weekend?"

I lied and told him Abby and I had studied all morning.

"Good. Then you can stay."

"I can't."

I quickly kissed him good-bye and headed to the door.

I thought he was reaching for the knob to open the door; instead, he grabbed me by the braid I'd worn all weekend. I was so shocked, all I could do was yell, "Hey!"

I fell backward onto the floor with Kip on top of me.

"What the hell are you doing?" I screamed.

He still had my braid in his hand. My entire head throbbed like some kind of halo from hell.

"God, I'm sorry. I was trying to stop you."

Mission accomplished. "Get *off*!"

He got up slowly and held out his hand to help me up. I half expected to find my braid on the floor, disconnected from my head.

He almost seemed as shaken as I was. "I don't know what happened."

That made two of us. I sat on the couch, shaking.

"Come here." He inched his way closer to me. Slowly, he unbraided my hair, brushed it out, and started to rebraid it. I hid my face from him as I cried. The way his fingers moved so quietly through my hair was almost more painful than the yank that had brought me to the floor.

"I'm so sorry," he said. "I just didn't want you to leave."

I nodded. All I wanted to do was go home.

He turned to face me. "You know that was an accident, right?"

I nodded again. The whole thing had happened so fast, I wasn't sure an instant replay could decipher what had just taken place.

He gently helped me up and handed me my bag and gift.

"You're at Goodwill tomorrow, right? I'll stop by with two mochas. We can sit outside during your break."

I could barely get any words out; I mumbled something inaudible and left.

The drive home was a daze. Kip was funny, generous, and smart, right? He was passionate and spontaneous—what just happened was an accident. Like two people bumping into each other on the street, a wrong-place, wrong-time collision.

I looked at the collage on the seat next to me. Kip had obviously spent hours on this gift. *That's* who he was. After the five months we'd been together, he certainly deserved the benefit of the doubt.

As I lay in bed that night, I realized tomorrow would be March 1. There wasn't a February 29 this year; today hadn't really been my birthday at all. I decided that's where I'd file tonight's incident with Kip: into a black hole of time, on a day I wasn't even born.

NOTES TO SELF:

● Stop fixating on what Abby would think about that night at Kip's a few weeks ago. It was a fluke.

● Tomorrow—ask Mr. Perez again about adding Basic Instinct to the tour—don't these people know their movies?

● The rumors are true—new club opening. Auditions next week! Kip has been great helping me prepare.

● I've been spacing on my new jokes lately—make sure to write them down.

● Things with Kip are fine.

I feel like such an asshole.

First the chilly reception back home in Napa,
then this. Becky's face—so shocked and hurt. I
wanted to pull my own hair out at the sight of her
crying. It's not like I didn't know it was wrong—of
course I did. It was over in a matter of seconds,
but still, it's unacceptable. The thought of her
leaving the apartment, thinking I was some kind of
monster . . .

It made me remember when Mom made the
decision to leave Dad. Selling all our furniture
while he was in Denver so she'd have enough money
to leave. (A roundabout way into the antique
business, to be sure.) I remember the smell of paint
and polyurethane while she, Zach, and I
refinished those pieces in the driveway late
Friday night for the yard sale the next day. We
were so <u>with</u> her, <u>wanted</u> her to leave, sick to
death of Dad's bullying too.

And now this . . .

What if Becky left and never came back? It kills me to admit how much I need her.

I've got to hold it together.

Won't make the same mistakes Dad did.

Can't let it happen again. <u>Won't</u> let it happen again.

I spent the next week perfecting my driver's license set for the new club. Fortunately for Kip, he didn't have to audition, since he'd worked with the owner, Tom, in Napa. Plus, he'd been doing well, even opening for Blues Traveler at San Francisco State last week. His place in the opening-night lineup was assured.

Even though Kip had been supportive, there were times I felt like I couldn't do anything right. I wanted to go to his niece's birthday party and the brunch at Yvonne's, Kip's friend from the frame shop. But unfortunately, I also needed (and wanted) to keep my two jobs and good grades. No matter how much work I did in the relationship, it was never enough. Making him happy was my top priority, but it seemed like the harder I tried, the more I failed. He thought the Lit paper I wrote for him on Fitzgerald wasn't interesting enough to hand in. When I couldn't figure out how to put a new cartridge in the printer, my lack of coordination was no longer adorable, but pathetic. My nickname went from Cinnamon Girl to

Red. I longed for April vacation—then summer—when Kip and I could spend more time together. That was probably all we needed.

At the audition, I recognized several booking agents from clubs in Silicon Valley. Some were from over the bridge in Marin, people I had pitched and sent tapes to before. A few of the men and women in the back could have been corporate bookers or scouts from L.A. The audition suddenly became much more important than getting one gig at a new club.

"Are you nervous?" Abby asked. "Because I am."

"Petrified."

"Maybe it'll make us better."

"Or worse."

We hung out in the greenroom and waited our turn. The small room was downright posh compared to the hallways and lobbies where we waited at most clubs. When I looked around, I realized Abby and I were the youngest performers by far.

Our friend Chris from Oakland walked offstage in a cold sweat. "Throw away everything you know about Rick's," he said. "Between the size of the room, the lights, and the sound, you might as well be doing your set on the moon."

I tried to tell myself auditions were part of the process, even bad auditions. I braced myself for the worst.

"Hey."

The familiarity of the voice shocked me. I whipped around. "What are you doing here?" I had made Kip and my parents *swear* not to show up.

Kip popped a stick of gum into his mouth. "Figured I'd lend some support."

"I asked you not to come!"

He waved me off, so I pulled him into the small hallway next to the bathrooms. "If I had wanted you here, I would have asked. I have a thing about auditions—you *know* this. I wouldn't let my *mother* come."

"I know you a little better than she does, wouldn't you say?"

The ludicrousness of his argument only made me angrier. "Kip, I'm begging you to leave. I'm on next. Please go."

He looked at me and smirked. "Nope."

"What?"

"I want to watch. I'm proud of you."

People buzzed by us. I told myself to stay calm. But I could feel the tears burning in my eyes.

"Kip, please."

When he reached for me, something inside me flinched. He pinned my arms back firmly, then kissed me.

"I'll be in the back."

Even with the good wishes and kiss, I could feel my anger rise. I had explicitly asked him not to come. He had promised he wouldn't. The next thing I heard was

Tom calling my name. I hit play on my tape recorder and took the stage.

My plan was to do the getting-my-license set I'd done in L.A. It was now my best set, but what came out of my mouth was miles from what I'd rehearsed so many times before.

I'm a big believer in not swearing onstage. As any comic will tell you, using the f-word is a surefire—yet cheap—way to get laughs. Besides, Rick insisted everyone in his club work clean. But my adrenaline catapulted an entirely different set from deep inside me. My words were electric, venomous; at one point, my lines came out with so much force I was actually spitting. I was Denis Leary without the cigarettes but with all the attitude. The lights, the acoustics, they didn't even dent my consciousness. What spewed forth was pure vent and bile. And is there anyone who *doesn't* hate the DMV? I torqued up the driving instructor rant, and the crowd loved it. I barely noticed the audience, but when I did, they looked aghast. By the end of my set, half the room jumped to their feet. The last thing I remember seeing was Kip's face in the back row, beaming.

⌁

I walked offstage, sure I was going to get sick. And if I heard "Congratulations" one more time, I wouldn't even make it to the bathroom.

The first person to catch up with me was Kip. "You're a shoo-in."

When Tom approached, I wanted to hide under the table. My set was a far cry from my audition tape. Despite the audience reaction, I didn't know what his policy was and feared the worst.

"You," Tom said.

Here it comes.

"You're in. It's a definite. Your friend Abby too. Stop by this week, I'll give you the details."

Kip looked at me as if to say "I told you so." I hurried to the ladies' room.

Abby stood at the sinks, waiting.

"Well, *that* was different."

"Don't worry. I won't be doing it again."

"That was so not *you*. But they loved it. Closet rage-oholics, all of them."

"The two of us are in," I said. "Tom just told me."

Abby put out her cigarette in the sink. "Really?"

We jumped up and down like two kids and planned how we would celebrate. But the whole time Abby talked, I was thinking of one thing. I remembered a time in fifth grade when I'd done a project on France for social studies. I had just thrown it together in twenty minutes, but for some reason my parents and teachers went nuts over it. The stupid thing even made it to the local news. I remember how embarrassed I was, getting so much praise for something I knew wasn't my best work. I felt the same way about my set tonight.

When we left the ladies' room, Kip was stationed outside. He congratulated Abby, then put his arm around me.

"Are we okay?" he asked.

"Besides the fact that you don't take what I say seriously?"

"Hey, I wouldn't have missed you for the world."

The three of us celebrated afterward with a late-night dinner of salads and tacos. When we got to my house, Kip asked if he could come in. I said it was too late, that I'd see him tomorrow. As much as the night had been a success, I was still confused by his behavior.

When he kissed me, he wouldn't let me go. "I love you," he said.

I nodded and slid out of the truck.

Inside, Delilah was writing checks at the kitchen table. She was dressed to the nines, this time as Shirley Partridge. When she asked me how the show went, I broke the news about Abby and me making the cut. She hugged me for a long time, then looked me in the eye.

"Was that Kip's truck in the driveway? Your mom's upstairs waiting to hear how it went—she's going to be angry if you let him go and not us."

I told her he surprised me, and I wasn't happy about it.

"Men who don't respect boundaries—that's not a

good thing." She stacked the envelopes in a neat pile. "You keep your eyes on that boy."

I was getting boyfriend advice—*good* boyfriend advice—from a six-foot-two-inch man with a shag and a miniskirt. And this was the most normal conversation I'd had all day.

I lay in bed awake for hours. There was no denying the night had been a success; no audience had ever responded to me that way before. My routine would never reach such an angry crescendo again. And what about Kip? Was he there to help me push past my own obstacles? Was that the point?

If so, he'd gone too far.

NOTES TO SELF:

● Do a postmortem on the audition tape—who <u>was</u> that girl?
● When I was getting dressed today, I noticed small black-and-blue marks on my arms. It was probably from that rough game of football with Christopher. Couldn't be from Kip at the club. Besides, he didn't grab me that hard.
● Don't tell Kip where my next audition is? Or rethink my own superstitions? After all, I did get the gig.
● No matter what Kip says, I am not writing that Lit paper over again.

From the Paper Towel Dialogues of
Kip Costello

I never should have grabbed Becky at the club. I just wanted her to be quiet and let me enjoy her show! What's wrong with trying to be supportive anyway? I'm not taking all the credit, but Becky's act has gotten so much better since we've been together. That set she did the night we met? Terrible! I'm proud of how far she's come.

But it was wrong to hurt her. I had to fake being happy over dinner the rest of the night. What was I thinking?!

I don't care how many problems we have, or if it seems like she's slipping away, blowing by me in every way—I can't let that happen again.

Delivered my sleigh bed—thanks a lot, Mom—to Snob Hill yesterday. This old woman is turning her sewing room into a space for her granddaughter (a little older than Hannah). I had two more deliveries to make, but this woman just wanted to <u>talk</u>. I had three glasses of lemonade and helped her hang a few pictures before I left. I actually didn't mind.

My father stiffed Mom on his payments this

month. She had to sell half the stuff in my room to make the rent. Heard from that coffee shop—I start on Monday. Hey, do two crappy jobs add up to one good one? I'm not going to tell Becky I'm making lattes—it's too embarrassing.

Hey, who put the stop-payment
on my reality check?

I'd only fallen asleep in classes a few times before—a result of late-night gigs—but I got caught snoozing twice in McDonnough's lab this week. Charlie nudged me so hard that I almost fell off the bench. That time I couldn't blame my comedy schedule; I was sleeping in class because I was barely sleeping at home. My mind just wouldn't stop— either planning ahead to ward off future fights with Kip or deconstructing our last argument to see what went wrong. Sometimes it seemed as if our passion had transformed itself into a weird kind of Hitchcockian tension. I constantly caught myself scanning each sentence before I spoke, looking for some kernel of trouble that might ignite Kip. The pressure of continuous self-regulation kept me staring at my poster-covered walls well into the light of dawn.

⌒

At Goodwill, I could feel someone staring at me while I priced a box of books. When I looked up, I spotted Peter, my old boyfriend.

As much as our relationship had rated a two on the maturity scale, it was still good to see him. His hair was matted in a pathetic attempt at dreadlocks; he never did get over that reggae thing.

"Hey, Beck! What's up?"

From the size of his smile, he was genuinely happy to see me. One thing about Peter—what you see is what you get.

"How's the comedy scene?" he asked. "I hear you're working all the time."

I told him I had opened Tom's new club, that I was even hoping to perform around the state this summer.

"I always knew you had it in you."

As he paid for the X-Men comic books, I looked him over. Maybe not the brightest or funniest guy on the block, but kind. And kind was moving up on the scale of important qualities lately. When he asked me to go next door for a coffee, I told Harold I was taking a ten-minute break. (But not without mentally checking Kip's schedule to make sure he was still at the frame shop.)

We ordered two mochas and sat in the corner of the restaurant. I asked if his sister was still working at the Web design company; he asked if my dad had seen the Stones when they stayed at the Ritz. (He had—Keith Richards ordered four bottles of wine and two Caesar salads.) I sipped my mocha and gathered up my courage.

"Pete? Can I ask you something?"

"Sure."

"When we were going out . . . did I used to make you . . . I don't know . . . angry?"

He seemed surprised. "Angry? I don't remember ever being angry at you. You're too easygoing to get mad at."

"Be honest. Did you ever think I was . . . incompetent? Stupid?"

He looked at me like I was flailing across the restaurant in a straitjacket. "Put it this way—I never thought you were stupid till you asked me *that*."

I made an attempt at a laugh. "Never mind. I'm working on this new routine. A whole self-deprecation thing."

"Self-*defe*cating might be funnier. Depends on the crowd."

I smiled in spite of myself.

"But you're the expert," Peter said. "I never could keep up with you."

This was certainly news to me.

As I finished my coffee, I felt relieved at how comfortable it had been talking to him. (Although I nervously checked my watch every two seconds, in case some unexplained phenomenon at the frame shop—a broken sprinkler system, a gas explosion—led to a surprise visit from Kip.) I was actually sorry when Peter said good-bye.

I spent the rest of the afternoon almost optimistic. If

what Peter said was true, maybe I wasn't part of Kip's problem at all. I could almost feel the muscles inside me relax.

The thrift shop often received phone calls from people who were moving or cleaning out their basements and wanted us to come over and pick up their stuff. The store policy was that we only accepted drop-offs, but in the case of the elderly housing down the street, Harold usually made an exception. So when Mr. Bowen called, saying he was moving to Albuquerque to live with his daughter, I told Harold I'd stop by on my way home to pick up his donations.

From the second I stepped into Mr. Bowen's unit, I was enveloped with Eau de Old Person, that curious combination of dandruff and mothballs that causes most people to hold their breath until they get back outside. But despite the aroma, Mr. Bowen's eyes sparkled.

"It would've taken me two taxi rides to get all this over there," he said. "Wouldn't have been worth it."

I told him it was no trouble, I was glad to help.

"My brother was supposed to take my collection, but his gout is so bad, he couldn't make it." He looked me straight in the eye. "I hope you find a good home for these fellas."

As I followed him to the back of the almost-empty apartment, I wondered what kind of items Mr. Bowen was bestowing upon us. The store had had good luck selling album or postcard collections, but we'd had boxes of old bottles taking up space for months.

We entered a small room off the kitchen, and I jumped when Mr. Bowen turned on the overhead light.

Rows of little glass eyes stared up at me with fixed expressions. I was surprised but moved farther into the room to get a closer look.

"You know anything about taxidermy?" he asked.

"Besides the fact that it's not on my list of career choices?"

"You say that now, but that's because you don't know enough about it." He handed me a stack of books: *How to Tan a Hide, How to Preserve Fur, How to Re-Create Natural Environments*. I took the books from his hand without looking at them because I couldn't stop staring at the animals.

"Been practicing this for forty years," he said. "Shame my brother couldn't take 'em."

Badgers, raccoons, minks, weasels—we might as well have been in Muir Woods instead of in the middle of the city. I picked up a squirrel mounted on a small piece of driftwood; it was holding an acorn between its tiny hands. It looked exactly like the squirrels that raided our bird feeder at home. Except that it was dead.

"Pretty good, huh?"

I told him how real it looked, that if I had seen it from across the room I would have sworn it was alive.

"It's all in the technique," he said. "These little fellas going to be safe with you?"

I said I would try my best to find them a new home, maybe even make a window display to show off his fabulous work.

"Well, I'm leaving for my daughter's tomorrow. They're all yours."

He helped me load the many boxes into my back seat and trunk. He also threw in a box of clothes and several ashtrays. I wished him luck in Albuquerque.

⌁

Even though it was in the other direction, I stopped by Golden Gate Park on the way home. More than once, the menagerie in the back seat made me jump when I glanced in the rearview mirror.

I pulled over near the Arboretum and got out of the car, still amazed by the lifeless mammals packed into my beat-up Toyota. I took out one of the boxes and sat on the grass under a willow tree.

I examined the opossum up close. How many years ago had he been roaming the city, raiding trash cans, wandering through neighborhoods? He used to be alive, used to *feel* things; now nothing penetrated his glassy stare. No more playing possum for you, little guy. Play dead often and long enough and people begin to think you are.

And right there I made the decision to keep Mr. Bowen's collection for myself. I'd turn the box of clothes over to the store, but this lifeless crew was coming home with me.

Back at my house, I hid the boxes in the root cellar—a small room in the basement where no one in the family had any reason to go. I covered them up with an old blanket and topped that with stacks of newspapers. I took off my sweater, threw it over the squirrel, and took him to my room. There was something about him that appealed to me—inanimate and numb. Maybe I'd bring all of them upstairs one by one. Who knows, I could possibly work them into my act or hide them all over the house for Christopher to find.

That night I slept like a log—like the one perched under the fox downstairs.

NOTES TO SELF:

● You have now entered the Twilight Zone.
● Forget about showing Kip or Abby my new posse—
they would not understand.
● Why does Tom want to set up a meeting with
Abby and me? Is he happy or unhappy with us? I
can't even tell.
● Finish that paper for Kip by Wednesday.
● Tell Mr. Perez to find someone else—I'm not
doing the Presidio tour again. Too boring.
● Idea for new set—taxidermied hecklers?
● I felt horrible pretending to be sick the night
Abby's parents were supposed to take us to dinner.
But Kip made me feel guilty about abandoning him
on a Saturday night; I didn't know what else to do.
And those fake coughs I kept doing in front of
Abby the next day—so lame.

As winter rolled into spring, our roller-coaster relation-ship continued. Kip and I would fight over something ridiculous—last time, let's see, a waffle? His words were often bullying, my responses strained. I felt like a suspect in some bad cop movie—"You have the right to remain silent. Anything you say will be misinterpreted, then used against you."

But all this fighting always resulted in passionate make-up sessions that would leave us buzzing for days. It was similar to the nervous excitement of waiting back-stage, then the burst of energy when the audience responded. Sometimes I thought we were confusing stim-ulation and tension for love, the two of us addicted to the adrenaline of the fights as much as the adrenaline of per-forming. But no matter how painful the argument, we never broke up. Even with all the angst, a day without touching base several times seemed inconceivable.

As much as our time together was a nerve-jangling high, I felt like there were so many parts of Kip's life he kept hidden from me. He'd been working a second job for a month before I found out about it, and even then it was only by accident when I stopped over one afternoon and caught him in his coffee shop apron. It upset me to know that he'd been too embarrassed to tell me.

I found myself going down to the basement often to visit my dead animal collection. I even went so far as getting a bigger book bag to hold a wider variety of my "friends." Their presence somehow reassured me.

Two giant pieces of good news arrived in the last few days of March.

First, I got into CalBerkeley and UCLA. (We're not going to mention Northwestern.) So now I had to decide between staying in the Bay Area with Abby and Kip or going to L.A. alone. I made dozens of pro and con lists but still had no idea how I could possibly make that decision in a month's time.

The second piece of news was even bigger. Abby and I had been wondering why Tom wanted to see us, but even in our wildest dreams, we couldn't have come up with this. He pulled out two videotapes from a huge pile on his filing cabinet. "I finally got around to watching your tapes. You two have been holding out on me."

I jumped in, recognizing the tapes we'd mailed out on my birthday. "They're good, right?"

"Better than the sets you did here." He looked at Abby.

"The handicapped parking bit—very funny." He turned to me. "And I loved the chocoholic thing."

I smiled. Not at the compliment, but at the fact that I had trusted my instincts on that routine and kept it in.

"So here's the plan," Tom said. "Memorial Day weekend—Comics Take a Road Trip. Three days, five gigs, ten high-school kids, right down the coast. Grand finale at the Improv."

The *Improv*? Was he kidding?

"I used to watch A&E's *An Evening at the Improv* growing up," Abby said. "It's what made me want to go into comedy."

"Yeah, well, A&E's got nothing to do with it this time." Tom leaned back in his chair. "This time we're running it on MTV."

The Improv? MTV? Abby and I barely succeeded in remaining in our seats.

"Here's the list," Tom said.

As soon as I spotted my name, I prayed Kip's was on there too. But the only name I recognized besides ours was Mike Leone from Burbank.

I didn't want to push my luck but felt I had to. "How about Kip Costello?" I asked. "You loved his political set."

"He's a good guy," Tom said. "But I wanted to mix it up a bit. I picked ten kids from all over the state—no substitutions."

He handed us our consent forms and sent us on our way.

Outside Abby and I raced through ideas about outfits, sets, and how many people we knew with VCRs who could make us copies of the show.

"Hey, did you recognize anyone on that list?"

I told her Mike Leone was the guy I'd met in L.A.

"You said he's nice, right? That should be fun."

"As long as I don't tell Kip. He's going to feel bad enough about this as it is."

"Keeping secrets from your soulmate now?"

I said Kip was just protective and I wanted to save him the aggravation.

"You mean save *yourself* the aggravation, don't you?"

I was elated by the possibilities ahead of me, but Abby was right—a part of me *did* worry about how Kip would take all this good news. Would he be supportive or angry? Toss a coin.

As ecstatic as I was, I dreaded telling him.

That night, before I left for Kip's, my mother cornered me in the laundry room. She'd been eyeing me all week, waiting for the perfect moment to have one of those mother-daughter interrogations she tried to pass off as a conversation. I'd been avoiding her like head lice.

"I didn't say anything before because I knew you had a lot on your plate," she began, "but now I want to know what's going on."

"What are you talking about? Everything's fine."

"Look, I'm no psychiatrist, but let's face it—you are going through *something*. I want to help, Beck, please."

I continued to fold my clothes, trying not to meet her gaze.

"Is it school? Because if it is, you shouldn't be putting so much pressure on yourself this late in the game."

I told her it wasn't school.

"Are you worried about the Improv? You remember our deal—when comedy starts taking away from the rest of your life, you're done."

I explained that my career was finally beginning to take off.

"Then it's got to be Kip," she said. "I don't want to pry; you're eighteen, in charge of your own body. But is he pressuring you?"

I knew she was concerned, but I somehow felt this tack was all about finding out if I was sleeping with him or not. I told her it wasn't Kip. I just wanted the conversation to *end*. Yet despite my better judgment I took the bait.

"Like you have a lot of experience in the relationship department." My voice had more fire than I'd intended. "You and Dad are so lovey-dovey, it's ridiculous."

She tried to hide her smile. "We've had a lot to work out over the years. We just never did the difficult stuff in front of you."

"Well, maybe you *should* have. Maybe my expectations in a relationship would be a little more realistic."

"So it *does* have something to do with Kip."

I hated having a lawyer for a mother.

"Can we just end this before I get a migraine? You know I hate it when you cross-examine me."

She leaned against the wall and folded her arms across her chest. "I consider you one of the smartest kids I know."

"Yeah, smart and funny, that's me."

"Then *act* smart. Ask for help when you need it."

"The only help I need right now is folding these clothes."

Frustration still filled her face, but she smiled anyway—Mom, always a trouper. "If that's what you need, you got it." She took the pile of socks and began sorting them.

I stood there fuming. Gee, Mom, so glad you asked about Kip! He's a great guy 90 percent of the time, I love him more than I've ever loved anyone, but sometimes he gets angry at me, and I don't know what I did to set him off. I'm spending more and more time worrying about saying or doing the wrong thing. Is that normal? Plus, I have to decide on my future in the next thirty days. And by the way, I'm also sitting in the dark with a bunch of dead animals. Does that meet with your approval? Maybe you have some handy tips about life and love that I can laminate—wallet-size—to help me sort through all of these feelings? *What did she want me to say?*

I told her I was late and headed to Kip's.

If it hadn't been so pathetic, I'd have put it into a routine—life handed you something amazing like the Improv gig, then turned around and had your mother torture you just to keep you on your toes. It took me the entire walk over to Kip's before I could shake off the conversation.

I waved to Kip's mom on my way up to his apartment; a tiny part of me was relieved that she was close by in case Kip overreacted to my news. (Which only made me feel guilty.)

"You and Abby at the Improv," he said. "That's beautiful. Affirmative action, even in the world of comedy."

"It's not just girls," I said. "Guys are going too."

"You're not seriously thinking of going on the road with these clowns, are you? They're just going to rip you off. You'll end up seeing your jokes in some *SNL* skit a week later."

"You're so negative!" I said. "How about if I get a big break? That could happen too."

"Not likely. Anyway I'm sure your mom will put the kibosh on the whole thing."

I told him my parents had approved, that Delilah had even volunteered to come along as chaperone.

Silence.

He finally spoke. "I can't believe you're thinking about going if I'm not."

I backpedaled like a monkey riding a bike at the circus. "Nothing is definite," I lied.

"Let's hope not. I mean, I would never go if they left *you* out."

"It's no big deal." Another lie.

"Just don't sign anything," he said. "Believe me, they see someone like you coming a mile away."

"Someone like *me?*"

"You know—young, naive. You better run everything by me if you don't want to get screwed."

I didn't respond. At this point, keeping the peace was more important than being heard.

NOTES TO SELF:

● Watch <u>The Graduate</u> for the CalBerkeley scenes.
Compare to the UCLA campus in <u>Scream 2</u>. Decide
on a school, already!
● Kip finally seems to be accepting the road trip—
he hid an L.A. guide in my book bag yesterday—
thank God, the chipmunk wasn't in there.
● An Improv gig—am I up for it? I've been feeling
like Ms. Stupid, Fat, Low Self-esteem. I still can't
believe they picked me.
● Maybe I should have said no to the road trip.
Forget it—that sentence did not just come out of
my pen!

From the Paper Towel Dialogues of
Kip Costello

It took every bit of willpower I had not to call up Tom screaming. I mean, Abby and Becky are funny, but anyone at Rick's would tell you that I'm a better candidate for the Improv. I don't want to sound like sour grapes—Becky works her ass off—but is there any reason I can't catch a break sometime?

I didn't mention anything to Becky about that guy Mike from L.A. I couldn't help it; I checked her e-mails—I wish she had told me he was one of the guys on the trip. I guess it's not that different than me not telling her about my job at that coffee shop; we're just trying to show each other the good parts of ourselves, not the insecure, embarrassed sides. It's like that first day she came over and I hid all my junk in the pantry. How do you know how much of your life to share? Okay, Beck not telling me about that guy from L.A. being on the road with her is worse than me not telling her about my lousy job. I mean, a cappuccino machine is not going to steal me away from her, but this guy . . . why is he e-mailing her already, all excited—doesn't he have a life?

Speaking of getting a life . . . what's with some of these guys in Thompson's class? It's such a big, stupid act—them pretending to be tough; me being tough in return—when we're all just trying to get through the day without being humiliated.

I ended up going to Mrs. Lawton's again. Poor woman has no one to talk to. I guess I don't either, 'cause I stayed there for two hours. I put those glow-in-the-dark stars all over the ceiling of the room she's fixing up for her granddaughter. Her face lit up more than the stars did when she saw them shine. Reminded me of Becky.

I moved the stacks of newspapers and crawled underneath the blanket to my little basement hideaway. It reminded me of camping, sitting inside the safety of my Girl Scout tent looking out the flaps for animals. Back then, if I'd ever seen this many wild creatures I would have huddled into my sleeping bag in fear. And if I'd known they were dead—forget about it. But now, these excursions were beginning to feel like a picnic with old friends. Last week the mouse accompanied me in my bookbag; this time, I chose the blue jay.

I used to have a handle on life, but it broke.

As I picked up the delicate bird, I heard someone coming downstairs. I shut off the flashlight and remained still.

"Becky, you down here?" Delilah asked.

I sat there silently.

"I know you didn't leave the house because your cell's upstairs. And damn, if that thing hasn't been ringing all afternoon."

I couldn't give in; it was too embarrassing to be caught down here red-handed.

"That crazy-in-love boyfriend of yours called three times, asked if you could stop by the frame shop. Rick called too, wants you to headline tonight."

Headline?

"I thought that might get your attention. I left you a note upstairs with the details—whenever you're done doing what it is you're doing down here."

I didn't know how Delilah navigated the basement stairs in those stilettos, but she did. I put the blue jay in my bag, covered up the animals, and waited a few moments before running upstairs behind her.

I read the note and dashed up to my room; I had just a few hours to get dressed, run through my set, and see Kip at work before the gig.

~

Headlining! A good time slot—nine o'clock—and twenty minutes instead of my usual ten. Boy, was I ready. My mother insisted I eat something, so my father whipped up an arugula and goat cheese salad with apple and walnut dressing. (I love him.)

When I got to the front door, Mom was standing there with her keys.

"You're coming?" I asked.

"Don't I always?"

"It's just, you don't have to anymore. Now that I'm eighteen, Rick's been letting us wait by the bar as long as we don't drink."

"But you're finally headlining!"

"I know, I just . . ."

"Would you rather I not come?"

"Well . . ."

"Becky, why are you tiptoeing around? Since when can't you just say what you mean?"

I took a deep breath. Okay, just be honest.

"Kip's working late. I was going to stop in and see him, then go to the club alone. Is that all right?"

"Of course it's all right. You don't need to treat me with kid gloves, you know." She handed me the keys, and I hugged her good-bye.

On the way to the frame shop, I practiced telling Kip about the gig. ENTHUSIASTIC—I'm headlining! LOW-KEY—Rick needed someone to fill in, I had nothing else to do. GOOD GIRLFRIEND—why don't I take the frame orders and *you* go perform? I shook myself out of it. Mom was right; don't tiptoe around, just *say* it.

Kip had been working since ten that morning; he looked exhausted and hungry. But when he saw me, he vaulted over the counter.

He held me close and kissed me. "God, the first good

thing in my day. I've got a break in fifteen minutes, we can go grab a sandwich."

"Rick called. He asked me to headline."

He picked me up a foot off the ground. "That's great. What time, twelve?"

"Nine."

I might as well have slapped him in the face. "You told him you'd take the *nine*? You know I'm doing a double shift."

"I know, but nine is what he had." I took Delilah's note from my bag. "See? Someone got sick at the last minute, and he wondered if I could help out."

"I can't leave now," he said. "We're mobbed."

I told him he didn't have to leave, that it was no big deal. I could see him trying to decide which words to choose next. Please, I thought. Be nice.

He wasn't.

"Is this it? I groom you for success so you can go off and perform on your own? Whatever happened to gratitude?" he whispered.

I apologized yet again. Bill, his boss, walked by and gave us the evil eye.

Kip suddenly grabbed an order form from the counter. "What we need to do is preserve this memorable occasion." He began to fill out the form. "Let's see—Becky Martin. Address, phone—know those by heart." He took

Delilah's note from my hands and began to rummage through the racks of frames. "Let's see, maybe gold—"

"Kip, can we just talk about this?"

"Or gold with a hint of green?" He held up two different frames. "Which one do you like better?"

"This isn't funny."

He continued to hold up the frames. In the long run, it was usually easier just to go along; I pointed to the frame on the left.

"Okay. Number fifty-nine. Now, we need a mat. . . ."

I stood between him and the counter. "This isn't about Rick's at all, is it? This is about the Improv."

"Oh, and that guy Mike you met in L.A.?"

"What?"

"Don't act all innocent—he's been e-mailing you for weeks." His voice attracted a few new onlookers.

He suddenly looked as if he was about to cry. I reached for his hand, but one of the guys in the back room walked by and Kip pulled away.

"No, you should go," he said. "Tonight Rick's, then the Improv, soon you'll have your own HBO special. You and Mike."

"Mike has nothing to do with us. I swear."

"Sure, new boyfriend all lined up and ready to go. Next!"

I could feel the familiar shame creeping up my face. "That isn't funny."

"The Improv's gone downhill anyway," he said. "No one wants to work there anymore." He moved around me and went back to the mattes. "What do you think— black, beige, or the dark green?"

"Can't you just *talk* to me?" I could feel the tears forming in my eyes. I blinked them back, determined not to make a scene. Several people in line looked over, and I lowered my voice.

"Well?" Kip asked. "Which matte is better?"

I stared him down, then finally answered. "Black."

"Nonreflective glass or regular? Myself, I'd go with nonreflective, this being such an important document and all."

He finished filling out the form with a flourish. "That'll be $68.47."

"I don't want a stupid frame and you know it."

He got in my face. "Do you mean to tell me you've been wasting my time all along?"

"No!" I shouted.

"Because I've got a big problem with someone wasting my time."

I looked around, hoping others weren't staring. A middle-aged woman waiting in line looked annoyed, but more with me than with Kip. I inched my way closer to him.

"I don't want to fight about this. I'll call Rick and tell him something came up."

He thought about it for a moment. "No, no—you should go."

My mind flashed to the conversation with my mother in the doorway. Was *I* the one making these discussions so complicated? I asked Kip if he was sure about me going.

"Yeah. Have a great set. Leave me a message and tell me how it went."

"Really?"

He smiled. "Absolutely."

I was getting whiplash from all the ups and downs in the conversation. I smiled back halfheartedly and turned toward the door. Kip's boss came by again, looking even more perturbed.

"Miss?" Kip said. "That'll be $68.47. You pay now, not when you pick it up."

Was he kidding? He pointed his head toward Bill, who circled by again.

Kip folded his arms and waited.

People in line began to turn around.

And stare.

I just wanted to make it out the door without a scene. Would do *anything* to avoid a scene. I took out my wallet and handed Kip my emergency credit card. He ran it through the register and gave me the receipt to sign. Then he took Delilah's note from the counter.

"We'll take good care of this," he said. "It'll be ready on Thursday."

Outside on the sidewalk, I burst into tears.

Why had he humiliated me like that? What was he trying to prove?

When I finally calmed down and opened my bag to put my credit card away, I saw the blue jay. Which made me start crying all over again. I suddenly remembered an old Lily Tomlin line—"If love is the answer, could you please rephrase the question?"

I looked at my watch and hurried to the car. If word got out I had bagged Rick at the last minute, I wouldn't work for weeks. I raced to the club.

In his familiar Buzzcocks T-shirt, Rick was a welcome sight. I had never realized how much I'd grow to appreciate predictability.

"You ready, Sunshine? Caitlin's on, then you."

I went to the ladies' room to compose myself. Block it out, compartmentalize. You can do this.

I threw Rick my half-opened bag and took the stage like a pro. With my anti-nostalgia set, I had a solid twenty minutes. Until something happened that hadn't happened in months.

I got heckled.

Some poor dope with a buzz on made the mistake of busting my chops onstage. I mean, who in their right mind heckles a comic with a mike in her hand? This guy was asking for me to bury him.

I obliged.

~

"The only thing I'm nostalgic for is somebody funny," the man yelled.

"Excuse me?" My set was clicking; I was completely in the zone. Couldn't this moron *see?*

"You heard me, honey. Your act stinks!"

The man and his friends sat right up front, begging me to spar.

"That's pretty funny," I told the man. *"Especially coming from a potbellied guy with pressed jeans trying to pretend he's not a tourist from the Midwest visiting San Francisco for the first time. Let me guess—you spent the day eating sourdough bread, then drinking hot chocolate at Ghirardelli's, right?"*

His friends laughed. *"You got it!"* one of them yelled.

"You probably came here from Iowa, wore your sweatsuit on the plane, finagled senior discounts even though you're only fifty-nine."

"Fifty-five—he just looks bad!" His friends were loving this. Easy to turn that around.

"So you gathered up your middle-aged cronies, all of you looking for something to distract you from your insipid little Corn Country lives. You traveled to the Big City, taking pictures of each other huffing and puffing up Lombard Street—'Wow! This really is the most crooked street in the world!' Walking around the Castro, hoping to see some gays so you can tell the fellas back home you saw two guys making out right in front of you. You and your friends grabbing each other's asses, acting out all those homoerotic urges you keep bundled up inside during your poker games back home. Then—something really original—listening to the audio tour at Alcatraz, you and your buddies take turns locking each other in the cells, more homoerotic tendencies to act out. Then what? Irish coffees at the Buena Vista? Can you get any more predictable?"

When the men got up to leave, they no longer looked full of bravado, just embarrassed and old.

"Oh, what's the matter? Can't take the heat? You'd rather shout out insults to a teenager from the safety of a darkened room, is that it? Hey, tell your friends at the diner back home you really kicked ass, humiliating a young girl onstage in San Francisco."

The guy and his friends headed to the door in silence.

"Good! Go, you big dope!"

I put the mike back in its stand.

"Stupid bastard."

Rick was in my face the second I walked offstage. "What the hell was that?"

Good question. "I am so sorry, Rick. I—I lost it."

"What, now that you've got a television spot lined up, you forget your roots?"

"Of course not!"

"You wait right here." He walked onstage to introduce Greg. When he came back a minute later, his ears were still burning.

"Putting hecklers in their place—fine. Making them sorry they ever opened their stupid mouths—great. But sending them out the door—*not* fine! You know how much money you just cost me in drinks? And if they go back to their hotel and say what a crappy time they had, I can forget about concierge referrals altogether. Not to mention that you performed five minutes instead of twenty. Now I've got to find somebody else to make up the time."

"I'll stay and do the eleven."

"Forget it. I don't want you here."

"Rick, come on! I'm sorry."

"And don't think I'm paying you."

"No, of course not."

"You're done tonight, Becky. Go home."

He shoved my bag into my hands. "And take Tweety

Bird with you. I'm not even going to ask what kind of good luck charm *that* is."

I stumbled into the street, mortified by my own behavior. I hit Abby's number on my speed dial and told her what happened.

"All Rick cares about is the register," she said. "The last thing he's worried about is that guy's feelings."

"It matters to me," I said. "I didn't get into comedy for this!"

"What do you think happened?"

I knew but didn't answer.

I had yelled at the wrong guy. The person I wanted to be screaming at was Kip. I didn't dare tell Abby about tonight's torturous incident with the frame.

"Look at the bright side," Abby said. "At least you worked on your improvisational skills."

"Stop it."

"Hey, if it's tourist season, does that mean we can shoot them?"

"Abby! When I talked about trusting my instincts, I didn't mean jumping all over some middle-aged guy in a one-way rant."

"We can work on that."

It was nice to hear the word *we*. She said there were worse things that could've happened and she'd see me tomorrow.

I drove downtown to the Marriott and the Hilton, two

hotels known for their tourist packages. I walked around the lobbies, not even sure what I would do if I saw the poor guy. Say I'm sorry? It made me realize the conversation I'd just had with Abby was the first one in memory where I hadn't made some sort of apology.

I was back home much earlier than my one o'clock curfew.

My mother was in the den watching *Casablanca* with the sound off, playing Joni Mitchell's *Ladies of the Canyon* in the background. "It lines up perfectly," she said. "'Big Yellow Taxi' is on when Rick gets in the car, I swear."

I sat down next to her on the couch. When she asked me how it went, I lied and said it was one of my best sets ever.

"You want some popcorn? I can make more."

I shook my head and sneaked under the blanket with her.

"Watch," she said. "I love this scene."

Rick was berating Ilsa for jilting him in Paris years before. Even with the sound off, his cruelty was visible on her face. Ilsa's humiliation was too much for me to bear. I crawled upstairs to bed.

I lay in bed for hours, staring at the movie characters on my wall—my own personal audience. I was embarrassed at my new form of comedy. Not just tonight's rant, which was unforgivable, but my sets in general. My jokes had turned increasingly angry. Sometimes it seemed like my relationship with Kip was fueling something negative and bitter inside me.

For once I didn't lose sleep worrying or playing what-if.

For once I stopped procrastinating and made a decision.

I was going to UCLA.

NOTES TO SELF:

● Beg Rick's forgiveness; he's still mad.
● Mom and Dad actually took my UCLA decision
well—Dad sent in the deposit.
● Surprisingly, Kip was okay with my decision too.
He vacuumed my car yesterday; I think he still felt
bad about the frame.
● Set up routine heckle practices with Abby so I
don't make the same mistake again.
● Finalize set for the Improv show. Focus on the
good things.

From the Paper Towel Dialogues of
Kip Costello

What was I thinking with that whole frame thing? Granted, Bill has been looking for an excuse to fire me, and I had to come up with something to look like I was working, but I never should've treated Becky like that. I canceled the order as soon as she left the shop. I've been on the receiving end of those humiliating feelings and wouldn't wish them on anyone. Yet that's just what I did to her.

Well, I certainly can't blame Becky for going to UCLA. The way I acted, I'm surprised she's not moving to Mongolia. I'll still be able to see her, it'll just be different. I had this whole scenario in my mind—the two of us living here, going to Berkeley, maybe finding a place on Telegraph. I blew that one.

I don't think either of us realize the stress we've been under. I got rejected at four out of my five schools, didn't get picked for the Improv gig. I'm working two jobs, almost flunked two classes—I know that's no excuse for how I acted. At least I didn't grab her this time—I hope I learned that lesson.

I've been thinking about the relationship a lot, trying to understand it. I know it sounds screwed up, but when things are good, it's like she's in control of the relationship; when things are bad, I am. It doesn't make any sense, but it's true. Half the time I wonder why she's with me. But if I let her know how great she is, she might leave. I don't want things to be bad, but I'm not comfortable with her running the show either.

How do other guys know what to do, what to say? Was I absent the day they handed out the instruction manuals?

A relationship is a lot like a hot bath. The more you get used to it, the more you realize it's not so hot. . . .

It was reassuring to watch Kip with his eighteen-month-old niece. He doted on her every gesture, changing her outfit when he thought she was chilly, warming her bottle in a pan on the stove. While Kip's brother, Zach, and sister-in-law, Susan, spent the day visiting museums with Alex, we gladly played parents for the afternoon.

Walking down to the waterfront, we admired the reflection of the three of us in a furniture store window.

"This will be us," Kip said. "We'll take our kid on the road, let her hang out in the greenroom on the *Tonight Show* while Mom and Dad blow the audience away."

"Yeah, right."

But our future *could* be amazing. If we ever got through all these ups and downs. Love/hurt. Love/fear. Love/pain. If we worked through *those*, maybe we'd be okay.

At Ghirardelli Square, we held up toys and stuffed animals for Hannah to enjoy. We hung on her every emerging word. At Fisherman's Wharf, we watched several street performers.

"Do you have to use a silencer to shoot a mime?" Kip whispered.

Later, we took turns feeding Hannah while sharing take-out noodles in the park.

An amazing day.

We walked back to Kip's with Hannah sleeping contentedly in the Snugli around Kip's neck. At the bakery next door, a woman lined up pastries in the window. As if he could read my mind, Kip went inside and returned with two chocolate croissants fresh from the oven. We climbed the stairs to his apartment, licking the warm chocolate from our fingers.

When I took off my jacket, two felt pens fell out of my pocket.

"I forgot—I got these for you the other day. For your paper towels."

He stared at the pens I gave him. "These aren't the kind I use."

"Black felt, right?"

"Well, they're black. And they're felt. But that's about all they have in common with mine."

Accommodate. Ease. Smooth over. I was finally getting a handle on the skills I needed in the relationship. I told him I'd use the pens myself and would pick the right ones up next time I was at the office supply store.

He shook his head, still disappointed.

"What's the matter?"

"Nothing." He tossed his keys in the bowl.

"What?"

He stood there as if deciding whether or not to get into it. "It kills me," he said. "I know everything about you, *everything*. How you like your chocolate warm, not room temperature. How you need it perfectly quiet to study, but only after you've listened to music playing full blast." He lowered his voice so he wouldn't wake Hannah, still sleeping against his chest.

"I pay attention. And you—the queen of detail in your act—can't even remember the pen you've seen me hold in my hand every single day for almost eight months."

I tried to lighten the tone. "Maybe I was focusing all my attention on you and not your pen."

"Maybe you weren't paying attention at all."

I couldn't believe it. We weren't fighting over me moving to L.A. or about our future or about Mike being on the road with me next week; we were fighting about a *pen*. "Come on," I said. "It's nothing."

"Obviously it is to you."

"Hey, whatever happened to 'It's the thought that counts'?"

"That's what's bothering me, the *thought*. I mean, what were you thinking? First it's going on tour without me, then it's going to school four hundred miles away, then it's not paying attention to the critical details of my life—"

"I've had a lot on my mind, okay?"

"I'll tell you what's *not* on your mind—me!"

I didn't want this to escalate; I wanted both of us to calm down. "Look. I had a really great day. But I've got to go."

"You're not leaving."

When I headed to the door, he tried to grab me. I moved out of his grasp quicker than I did last time. But when I stepped aside, he grabbed my hoop earring instead of my braid, ripping it right from my ear.

I yelped in pain and shock at seeing the blood spurting from my earlobe. My stomach churned when I reached up and felt the delicate flesh torn in two.

Kip threw my hoop across the floor. "Look what you made me do!" With his raging voice only inches from Hannah's face, she awoke with a wail. He pushed me to the ground, Hannah swinging from his torso in her Snugli. She must have thought Kip was swinging her intentionally because she stopped crying and went back to sleep.

I couldn't contain the bleeding; the shoulder of my shirt was covered in blood. "I have to go to the emergency room." I couldn't believe how calm my voice was, since my insides were screaming.

Kip grabbed his keys and said he'd take me.

"No!" I felt like I was going to be sick, the taste of chocolate still fresh in my mouth.

"Of course I'm taking you." He took one of Hannah's bottles from the fridge and stuck it in her diaper bag. He reached into the pantry and handed me a towel for my ear.

"Beck, come on. You'll get there faster if I drive you."

He was right, of course. I climbed into the truck and leaned as far away from him as I could.

～

On that ride to the emergency room, did I worry about an ugly scar? Yes. About what I would tell my parents? Absolutely. But what I worried about more was how this could have happened again. What kind of an idiot was I? I cried most of the way to the hospital.

Thankfully, the waiting room wasn't crowded. When the doctor saw my ear, he recommended three stitches. While he cleaned the wound, he asked me what had happened.

Before I could make up a story to answer the question, Kip went into a lively routine about Hannah trying to grab my large hoop earrings all day, how while Kip and I were kissing, she had reached up and yanked. He acted the whole thing out, imitating Hannah's scrunched-up face and chubby fists, my shock, Hannah's joy at finally retrieving the glistening wire. When he finished, I thought the doctor and two nurses were going to burst into applause. Even Hannah bounced in her Snugli with glee. By the time we left the ER, I almost believed the story too and knew it would be the version I would tell my parents.

As I walked down the hospital corridor, a thought hit me like lightning.

Kip and I had had the perfect day, projecting ourselves into the future, pretending to be husband and wife. Like one of the Zen epiphanies Abby and I tried to foster with our cards, I finally *got* it. This *is* my future, I thought. Lies. Injuries. Emergency rooms.

This *is* the husband he'd be, the wife I'd be.

Abused.

For the first time, I saw the situation for what it was. The flash card finally worked—I was awake.

In the parking lot, I didn't get into Kip's truck.

"It's over," I said. *"We're* over."

"Becky, come on. It was an accident and you know it."

"Maybe the first time was an accident. But this . . ." I could feel my tears burning. "I can't do it anymore."

When Kip walked toward me, I moved. "Get away from me."

"I'm sorry," he said.

"You need help."

He leaned against the truck and bounced Hannah against his knee. "If you stay with me, I'll get help. The two of us—"

"There is no us," I whispered. "I'm out of here."

"Becky—"

"Not another step, Kip. I swear to God." I turned and ran toward the street.

~

For the next hour, I walked through the city like a zombie. I thought about my mother's careful comments, about Abby's concerns. I felt full of shame for letting myself get sucked into something like this. Incompetent and pathetic, that was me. Was I so desperate for love that I'd put myself in danger? Between the shame and the pain in my ear, the nausea never let up.

I walked for hours, finally resting on a bench down by Fisherman's Wharf. I had been here earlier in the day, hopeful and optimistic. Now I felt ridiculous. I looked across the bay to Alcatraz. I couldn't tell if I'd just escaped from prison or entered one. One good thing about denial—it hurts a lot less than the truth does.

On the way home, I passed the shop where Kip had learned to braid my hair. Marla sat at the receptionist's desk booking an appointment. She waved when she saw me through the window; I walked into the shop.

"Here she is. The girl with the prettiest hair in San Francisco."

"Cut it off," I said. "All of it."

"You're kidding me, right?"

As an answer, I walked to the row of sinks and sat at the first one. Marla shrugged and took an apron from the cabinet.

Kip loved my hair. Loved to brush it, loved to reach across the table at the diner to touch it. Of course, some sick, screwed-up part of him thought it was a handle made for grabbing my head. I needed something tangible to tell myself I was serious, that Kip and I were over. No more wavy tresses, no more dangling earrings, no more toddlers taking the blame for an eighteen-year-old man.

Marla led me to her chair. I took the scissors from her hand. "May I?"

I lifted up a hunk of hair and cut.

"Honey, honey, let a professional do her job."

But I wouldn't give her the scissors. Through the mirror, I watched the other patrons stare at me as I hacked off my hair in giant clumps.

"I take no responsibility for how this comes out," Marla said.

Only when my hair was a few inches long did I give the scissors back to Marla.

She reached over to the next station and handed me a box of tissues. "Oh, sweetie," she said. "Don't cry. That's the good thing about haircuts—they all grow out."

I took a handful of tissues and wiped my teary face.

The last thing on my mind was my hair.

NOTES TO SELF:

HOW COULD I BE
SO STUPID?!?

From the Paper Towel Dialogues of
Kip Costello

Something horrible happened.

No, that's not true.

I did something horrible.

I was shocked when I saw Becky's ear. The earring in my hand felt like a smoking gun. I DIDN'T MEAN TO HURT HER! She was leaving, and I was trying to stop her. If someone had asked me "Hey, do you want to tear off your girlfriend's earlobe today?" do you think I would have said yes? I had to put on the happy act for my mother, Zach, and Susan when I got back from the hospital. (It didn't work; Mom asked me ten times what was wrong.) Then I turned up the music loud, sat in the pantry, and cried. I know this is all my fault, but how can I make things better if there's no relationship left to fix?

We can't be over; we just can't.

Whatever happened to second chances, to working things out? I've got work to do—I know it— but it's not fair for her to keep leaving whenever things get difficult.

They're not just words, Beck, I really mean them—I am so, so sorry.

Mrs. Lawton called the shop today and ordered that kid's rocking chair Mom's had around for months. It's a good thing her eyesight is bad so she couldn't see my puffy eyes while I helped her rearrange the room. I lost my girlfriend, I wanted to say. I tried so hard to hold on to her that I hurt her. I need help. Tell me what to do. Somebody? Anybody?

But how on earth could Mrs. Lawton possibly know how to fix the situation, when I can't even begin to understand it myself?

Why didn't I tell my parents about the violence?

Shame? Not wanting to hear "I told you so"? Or in my worst fantasy, my mom going into attorney-from-hell mode and suing Kip, pressing charges? I avoided my mother for the next few days, as if she'd be able to read my mind with some maternal X-ray vision.

I decided not to tell anyone Kip and I had broken up. I'd just pretend to keep meeting him and let the relationship die a slow death.

Like *I* was doing.

I used the Hannah story to explain my stitches, used the Improv gig as justification for my hair. My mother asked so many questions, I thought it was a deposition. But she actually loved my haircut. (She'd been begging me to cut it for years.) Delilah seemed a bit suspicious with both stories but, thankfully, didn't add to the cross-examination.

I wanted to do one thing.

Sleep.

I slept as soon as I got home from school, slept so late in the morning, Christopher had to poke me with his toy spaceship to wake me up.

I changed the number of my cell phone. (The old number had thirty-nine unplayed messages on it, all from Kip.) I deleted his e-mails without opening them; I changed my password too. Every bite of food, every conversation took an enormous amount of effort. I felt diagonally parked in a parallel universe.

A few days afterward, I bagged school and hung out at Fort Point, one of the stops on our *Vertigo* tour. I envisioned Madeleine hurling herself onto the rocks below. For the first time I actually considered re-enacting the scene from the movie. I thought about Judy doing everything to make Scottie happy, how it never was enough.

I wondered what I should do about the Improv. Sure, the haircut would look okay, but that wasn't the real problem.

I didn't feel like being funny.

I had my material down but didn't know if I could get up the attitude and energy I'd need by next weekend.

⟿

I scoured the Internet for information on abuse (deleting any e-traces when I logged off—I'd learned that lesson).

There was a strange, sick comfort in seeing how many other girls were in my situation. But even looking at the "facts" didn't begin to help me make sense of what had happened.

My feelings fluctuated as if I were channel-surfing my own psyche. ANGER—I hate him! He's an animal, should be put away! CONFUSION—was it me? Did I do or say things that brought out the beast in him? HURT—didn't he love me? Was he lying when he said he did? What will I do without him? But most of all, SELF-LOATHING—only an idiot would let herself get into this situation. Couldn't I see the signs? *What is wrong with me?* These were the questions I asked myself over and over as I sat in the basement staring at the unblinking eyes of my animals.

～

Folding sweaters—left sleeve, right sleeve, back to front. My Goodwill job kept me sane. But it was only a matter of time before the inevitable happened. It took five days until I heard the familiar "Hey."

Kip's voice sent a shock from the base of my spine to my brain. I'd been watching the door all week, knowing Goodwill would be the best place for Kip to try and see me. I mumbled something about being busy without looking up from the pile of sweaters.

"Your hair looks amazing." He reached out to touch it, then stopped himself.

"This had nothing to do with you," I lied. "I just needed a change."

"Well, you succeeded on that count."

In spite of myself, his opinion mattered. "Does it look bad?"

"No! I told you, it looks good." He smiled, but I didn't smile back. "How's your ear?"

"It's a part of your body you never think about until something goes wrong. It hurts like hell." I finally looked up to meet his gaze, but I hadn't anticipated the block of sadness that hit me when I saw him. He was unshaven and looked like he hadn't slept in days.

He handed me a present wrapped in the beautiful paper from the frame store.

"I don't want a present," I said. "I want you to leave."

"It's for Christopher. His birthday's this week, right?"

Of course he remembered. Christopher had asked me several times if Kip was coming to his party. I had lied and told him Kip was out of town.

"Thanks, but you have to go now."

"There's something I have to tell you," he said.

"I don't want to hear it."

"It's just . . . I was going to surprise you. Before we broke up, I mean. I booked gigs in Santa Cruz, Carmel, and L.A. so we could see each other while you were on tour."

"So you could check up on me."

"No, I swear. I had the whole thing planned—we were going to play L.A., hang out on the beach in Carmel. It was supposed to be a nice surprise. I thought you'd actually *like* having me around. But now . . . I can understand if you don't even want to be in the same city as me. I'll cancel the gigs if you tell me to. I mean it, Beck."

My feelings continued to channel-surf, but part of the reason I didn't want Kip near me was because I didn't trust *me*, not him. Even after the trauma of the emergency room, I knew there was a *chance* I might fall back into the relationship, buoyed by hope and good intentions. To be honest, it was more than that. During these past five days, it felt as if a piece of me had stayed behind with Kip in that ER parking lot. Sometimes it seemed almost easier to be with him than to move on without that missing piece. I *knew* I shouldn't be with him, but leaving felt like swimming against the path of a well-worn tide.

On the practical side, it would be professional suicide if Kip canceled those gigs on such short notice. Booking agents had long memories; it didn't seem fair to ask him to cancel his shows just because we'd be performing in the same cities. I told him I'd think about it.

He left the store, stopping on his way out to say hello to Harold. Kip was a nice guy; people liked him. But I didn't want to take the chance of seeing him again, especially with so much at stake. I also didn't want to make him turn down three big gigs for me. If only we could do our shows without running into each other, without the possibility of hooking up on the road. I needed to safeguard myself, make sure Kip didn't try to weasel his way back into my life.

There was one way Kip could keep his professional reputation intact, and I would be guaranteed not to see him.

I'd come clean and tell Abby.

"He what? He *hit* you?"

"It was more like grabbed."

"More than once?"

I immediately backpedaled and told her the first time had been an accident, that this last time he hadn't intended to nail my earring. "It's over," I said. "Just let it go."

"He sent you to the emergency room? You were so wigged out that you cut your hair? And now you act like it's no big deal?"

"Would you stop being so dramatic? It's done," I

whispered. That's all I needed, another scene, this one in a pizza parlor.

"I don't think you're taking this seriously enough."

Scene or no scene, I lost it. "Can you cut me some slack here?" My words came out much louder than I'd intended. "I never should have said anything!"

"Yeah, that's been working well for you so far."

"Look, I just gave up the one person on the planet who meant everything to me—don't act like I'm not taking this seriously. Can't you at least give me some credit for working this out on my own?"

"What, so you can be the first woman in history who does?" Her eyes began to well up. "Why didn't you tell me? God, the thought of him hurting you . . ."

"Disaster averted, okay? Things are fine. We're going on tour tomorrow, we're playing the Improv! School's almost over. Can we just try to focus on the good things?"

I nervously played with the meditation beads around my neck. Telling Abby now felt like a giant mistake.

"Well, I'll tell you one thing—if he's going to be nearby, I'm keeping you under lock and key."

"Good, I want you to."

Her expression softened. "You really don't trust yourself, do you?"

"How can I trust myself? I've been making bad decisions for months. I want somebody else to be in charge for a while."

She blotted the grease from her pizza with a napkin. "Well, stop worrying. Things are going to be fine. I'll make sure of it."

I nodded and hoped she was right. But the chances of anything being fine right now seemed slim at best.

I got up my nerve to take the conversation even further. "I hope you don't look at me differently now, like I'm some kind of victim."

She looked surprised. "But you *are* a victim, can't you see that?"

I was sorry I had brought the whole thing up.

NOTES TO SELF:

● Pack enough clothes to change several times if I have to.

● Answer Mike's e-mails—I seem rude.

● Don't check the Internet to see what clubs Kip is playing.

● I'm still not sure if it was smart telling Abby; she's gone kind of Gestapo these last few days. If telling Mom will be anything like telling Abby, forget it!

● I've been thinking about Kip all day. Proceed with the lobotomy, Dr. Frankenstein; you have my permission.

● Focus, focus, focus. Fine-tune that college application set till it sings.

From the Paper Towel Dialogues of
Kip Costello

Talk about making a change! I almost didn't recognize Becky with that haircut. I was bummed, but think I did a good job of saying it looked nice. She said it had nothing to do with that afternoon with Hannah, but I don't believe her. I was too embarrassed to tell her that I talked to one of the counselors at school about what happened. He turned me on to this Batterer Intervention Program running every ten weeks right at the school. (I guess a lot of guys have lost their instruction manuals. Who knew?)

The first session got me thinking about power and control. I feel bad about some of the stuff that happened with Becky—okay, correction— some of the stuff I DID. When I remember making her buy that frame, I actually break into a sweat. And the earring, well, I'll sit in support groups till I'm eighty if I have to—<u>that</u> will never happen again.

I'm glad Becky e-mailed me to keep the gigs; that guy in Carmel would've bitten my head off if I'd canceled. She always thinks about other people's needs before her own; that's just how she is. I planned this whole trip to surprise her—but I'm taking a bath with the motel and gas bills. Good for the résumé, not the wallet. Who knows, maybe if Becky and I can see each other, we can work on patching things up. I'm still hopeful for us; will do anything to get her back.

Tom had hired a small bus and driver so the ten comics and two chaperones could all travel together.

"Is this a special-ed bus?" Delilah put down her two suitcases and boom box, then placed a hand on each hip. "Because I don't think there's enough room."

I told her we might have to jettison some of her wardrobe. The comment did not go over well.

"Hey, Becky!" I turned around, right into Mike's hug.

"I left you three messages," he said. "I wanted to hook up with you before the trip."

I apologized, making up a story about an answering machine with a mind of its own.

"I like your hair," he said. "You can really see your face now."

"I'm not sure that's a good thing." I introduced him to Abby and Delilah to take the attention off me.

"Did you hear who's hosting the show at the Improv?" he asked.

I had just assumed Tom would emcee, the way he did at the club. Mike said it wasn't him.

"As long as it's not Carrot Top," Abby said.

Little did she know that on our bad days, that had been Kip's new nickname for me.

"Are you ready for this?" Mike asked. "Jimmy Fallon."

This new information set off a flurry on the bus.

"I love, love, *love* him," Abby said. "It's going to be the best night of our lives."

By the time we reached Santa Cruz, our voices were hoarse from all the talking and laughing. We checked into the motel, then hit our rooms to rest for that night's show.

―⚡―

Abby and I lay on our separate beds, staring at the tiled ceiling.

"This trip would be totally different if you and Kip were still together," she said. "You'd be tense, watching every word coming out of your mouth, looking over your shoulder—"

"It wasn't that bad."

"Sure it was, you just couldn't see. I'm so glad you can relax and enjoy the weekend."

"If you stop nagging me about Kip I might be able to." I could never in a million years have told her that I'd answered Kip's last few e-mails. He had wondered which jokes I was doing for the Improv show and had come up with a killer punchline for the SAT joke. He had also told me about this batterer group at his school, said he was committed to getting help. For a minute there, it made me wonder if I did the right thing telling Abby.

I grabbed my toilet kit and told her I was taking a shower.

When I came out of the bathroom later, Abby was holding something in her hand.

"I went into your bag to borrow a shirt . . . I don't . . . what is this?"

"A squirrel?"

"I can see that. I'm just wondering why you have it."

"It's a long story."

She leaned back. "Continue."

I told her about Mr. Bowen and his taxidermy collection.

"You *kept* them? How many do you have?"

"I never really counted." That was a lie. There were thirty-four.

"There's a fine line between a hobby and mental illness," she said. "What are you going to do with them?"

I sat down next to her on the bed and took the squirrel from her hands. His eyes seemed familiar, and I smiled. "I don't know. Bring them to Goodwill, I guess. That's where Mr. Bowen thought I was taking them."

She reached over and touched the squirrel's fur. "We should think of something more original than that."

"When I'm ready," I said, "you can set your sick little mind to work."

"Yeah, *my* sick little mind."

I put the squirrel back in the bottom of my bag and took out a shirt for Abby.

~

The thirteen of us traipsed over to the restaurant across the street from the motel for dinner. I felt bad for the waitress—with ten of us trying to be the funniest one at the table, it was a wonder she got our orders in at all.

Afterward, Delilah worked her makeup magic (although Mike politely declined the eyeliner), and we headed to the club.

"Whoa! Check it out!" Mike said.

Tom told us they were taping tonight's performance as a rehearsal for Sunday's gig at the Improv. We all leaned out the window on the right side of the bus to see camera crews, TV trucks, and two giant spotlights crossing the sky.

"Now *this* is what I'm talking about." Delilah rummaged through her bag for her tiara.

"One thing about Delilah," Abby said. "She knows how to make an entrance."

And when Delilah descended the stairs of the bus as a radiant June Cleaver, those photographers had a field day.

"You ready?" Mike asked me.

"I was until I saw all this!"

Mike asked what my routine was about. I told him since this was a young crowd, I was doing my college application routine. He was bringing out a set of characters, Martin Short–style. I couldn't wait to see him.

Abby opened up her bag and held up one of the flash cards.

BE HERE NOW.

As opposed to the club down the street, watching Kip perform his set.

ARE YOU HERE OR SOMEWHERE ELSE?

I took a deep breath along with her.

I'm here, I thought. And I'm ready to go.

NOTES TO SELF:

● The college application set <u>killed</u>. That guy in the front was actually hitting the table at the Sanskrit/transcript joke—thank you, Kip.

● Jimmy Fallon, here I come.

● We watched the rehearsal tape in Tom's room the next morning. I was worried about my hair, but it looked okay.

● Next road trip, don't pick a roommate who gets up at 5 a.m. to meditate.

● I don't think it was a mistake to give Kip my new cell number. He's only called once, wants me to concentrate on the tour. He seems really serious about changing.

The other comics on the tour were funny, friendly, and great to hang out with.

But it wasn't like being with Kip.

I kept pulling out my notebook and reading through the entries from the past few months. "How could I be so stupid?" "Why ask for trouble with Kip?" None of the entries, however, deterred me from returning to the good memories—the way Kip threw back his head and howled during the old *Batman* TV show, the way he knew 99.9 percent of the words to every song on the radio, the way the orange gum he chewed made kissing him taste like eating a Creamsicle.

I knew breaking up was the right thing to do, was still angry about my ear (and hair). Still . . . I'd be lying if I said I didn't miss him, especially during this tour.

Needless to say, I shared none of these thoughts with Abby. But I did begin to return all his calls and e-mails behind her back.

The day before the big Improv gig, we hung out in Santa Barbara at the beach. I told Abby Kip was in L.A.

"No, he's not. He's performing here tonight. He's staying at the Seaside Motel."

"What?"

"I figured you might try to lie about where he is, then go and meet him." She squirted sunscreen on her legs. "So I did a little detective work."

Part of me was in awe of her resourcefulness, another part was furious my motivations were that obvious.

"You're wrong," I lied. "He changed his plans and drove to L.A. this morning." I took the bottle of sunscreen from her hands, applied it, then settled onto my towel. "But I'm over it—you don't have to worry."

A few hours later, between running on the beach and bodysurfing with Mike, Abby shifted her attention away from me. It was easy to break from the group and meet Kip for a few minutes at the restaurant up the street.

We hugged each other awkwardly, not sure what to do with our hands.

"The review in Santa Cruz was great," I said. "You really should be on this tour with us."

"Tell me something I don't know."

But when I looked up, he shrugged good-naturedly.

"I'm trying to make my own luck. I'm actually thinking about recording a cd, maybe setting up a Web page."

I told him they were great ideas.

"Your show's at nine, right?" he asked. "I'm doing the midnight show right down the beach. I'd love it if you came."

I'd thought about it, of course, wondering if it would be okay to watch him perform. I suggested bringing Abby.

"Bring the whole bus," he said. "I need all the laughs I can get." He reached across the table for my hand, but I pulled it away.

The rest of the conversation flowed as if we'd never broken up. What jokes worked, how we did on our finals, making plans for school in September. I had to constantly remind myself why I had left the relationship.

I checked my watch and told Kip I'd call him later.

On my way back to the pier, I remembered an experiment Charlie and I had done in physics class using centripetal and centrifugal force. Because of budget cuts, the experiment was downgraded from a motorized desktop carousel to two balls connected by a piece of string. Charlie might as well have been playing with a yo-yo for all the good he did; I ended up writing the report alone: *Centripetal Force—objects seeking center.* I wasn't even sure it was love that connected Kip and me anymore, more like a physical force propelling us together. Like two bodies locked in orbit, we had no control over our direction. Never seeing Kip again seemed as impossible as defying the laws of nature.

By the time I reached my friends, I knew I'd be going to Kip's show.

All I had to do was get rid of Abby.

—

That night Mike was a bit off but chalked up his mistakes to nervousness. An agent from L.A. gave Abby her card after the show, hopefully a precursor of what was in store for the rest of us. My set was rock-solid; if the Improv show the next night was as sharp as this one, I'd be more than happy.

When we got back to the motel, it was time to implement the plan I'd spent hours strategizing. I waited until Abby called home, then knocked on Delilah's door.

"Abby and I are turning in. We're beat."

"That makes three of us. See you tomorrow, honey."

I said good night and went back to my room. Then I told Abby that because of the five-o'clock alarm going off, I would sleep in Delilah's room. I took my toilet kit and pajamas.

"Are you sure?" she asked. "I can set the alarm softer if you want."

I yawned and said I'd be fine on Delilah's spare bed.

I would only be gone a few hours, then would sneak back into our room while Abby was asleep. In the morning I'd tell her Delilah snored so I came back. I shut off the light and walked toward Delilah's room. I kept going, past her room, past the vending machines, straight to the main road, where I caught a cab to Kip's club.

⌇

I had missed seeing Kip perform these past few weeks. Boyfriend or not, he was one of my favorite comics to watch, hands down. He finally had perfected the antique store set; his joke about the two-thousand-dollar vase his mother scored at a yard sale for three bucks finally came together.

He was beaming when he reached the table.

"I didn't see you—I thought maybe you decided not to come." He looked around. "Where's Abby?"

"I came by myself. I've got to be back soon, though."

"No problem. I can drive you."

What we didn't talk about that night was actually more important than what we did. As we discussed the clubs and the road, I could almost hear another conversation right below the surface of our words. *I miss you. Can we ever fix things? Is the damage irreparable? Can I trust you again? Will the support group work?* It was as if those words floated in thought balloons over our heads while we talked about managers and booking agents.

"I've got a surprise for you," Kip said. "I was going to mail it to you when I got back to the city, but I can't wait."

He slid a cd case across the table.

I told him I'd really missed his music.

He took out his Discman, loaded a cd, and placed the earphones on my head.

It was our show in Santa Cruz from the night before.

"How . . . ?"

"I knew you didn't want me at the show, so I had the sound guy record the whole set. Then I burned it on cd. It's all there—you, Abby, that guy Mike."

I hit the forward button until I found my routine.

"Oh my God! Wait till the others hear this!"

"I brought my laptop with me, so I burned ten copies." His smile was huge. "I knew you'd be excited."

I nearly dove over the table to hug him. The hug led to a kiss, which led to another. I told myself to stop. This was not in the plans.

I fumbled with the cd, then told Kip I had to go. He offered to drive me back.

"No, no. I can take a cab."

"What are you talking about? It's late. Come on."

I gathered up my stuff. This was *Kip,* not some mass murderer.

As we drove toward my motel, I didn't want the ride to end. For the first time, I felt Kip was being honest with me about his life. He talked about what an outsider he felt like at school. He talked about the support group, how he'd been terrified to walk into the room at first, but how he now looked forward to it.

"It's like A.A., I guess. Sitting around telling stories about how you screwed up. But I'm hoping since my girlfriend was born on a Leap Year, I don't have to go through all twelve steps."

This was the part of the relationship that still remained an aching hole inside me. Along with giving up the abusive boyfriend, I'd also given up the person who knew me best in the world, right down to my old routines. It seemed an unfair trade-off for anyone to make.

"Hey," he said. "My motel's the next street over. Let me get you those cd's."

"If you've already made them," I said. "Abby and Mike will go nuts."

He smiled, turned into the parking lot, and shut off the truck. "You're not going to sit here, are you? I don't think it's safe."

He was right. It was late, and I didn't know the neighborhood. I followed him to the door closest to his truck.

As he put the key in the lock, my body involuntarily flinched. Just a small, almost imperceptible twitch in my stomach. I told myself not to worry, that we were only getting the cd's, that he'd been on his best behavior, that the support group was obviously working.

As a matter of fact, I was sick of being cautious,

thinking something bad would happen. I decided to ignore the fearful instinct and go with another instinct instead.

When we got inside, I jumped him.

It was one of those scenes straight out of the movies—clothes flying, tripping over shoes, collapsing onto the bed.

We had a lot of catching up to do.

We sat there sharing a bag of potato chips from the vending machine outside, watching an old *Mary Tyler Moore* episode. Neither of us wanted to leave.

Then my cell rang.

I excused myself and took it in the bathroom.

"Where are you?" Abby asked.

Don't panic. Stick with the plan. "I'm with Delilah," I said. "What's wrong?"

"I don't know. I woke up and realized you could've been lying to me."

"Abby, it's the middle of the night."

"I know. And I know how Delilah freaks when her beauty sleep gets disturbed, so I didn't come pounding on the door. But I just got so *worried*."

"Well, don't," I said. "I'm going back to sleep."

"You sure you're okay?"

"Stop worrying! I'm fine!"

I hung up and threw the phone in my bag. I didn't

want to get caught; I'd have Kip drive me back in case Abby woke up again.

I came out of the bathroom and jumped back on the bed.

"Everything okay?"

"Abby thought I had her wallet." It was amazing how good I had become at lying.

Kip ran his hand through my still-short hair. "I can bring you back if you want."

"That'd be great."

I kissed him.

He kissed me.

The next thing I knew, another half hour had gone by. I told him I had to leave.

Kip handed me the cd's; I put them in my bag with my stowaway pajamas and toilet kit. (Not to mention the squirrel.)

When I looked up, I saw something shift in his face.

"Abby," he said.

"What about her?"

"She didn't lose her wallet."

"What are you talking about?"

His head dropped toward his chest. "You told her."

"Told her what?"

"About me, about my problem."

"No. No, I didn't."

He looked as deflated as I'd ever seen him. "That's why she called. Did you tell her?"

Which answer would make him less angry?

"Be honest with me!"

"I didn't tell her anything."

"You're lying!"

I grabbed my bag and went for the door. This time, with no hair or earring to grab, he pulled my arm and yanked me to the ground. The stained orange rug burned against my cheek.

"I'm doing all this work for you—for us—and you go tell Abby like it's some piece of gossip?"

Say anything; just get out. "She *guessed*. I told her it was nothing, that you had it under control."

"Do I look in control right now?" He pressed his knee into my back, pinning me to the floor. "Christ, Becky—why?"

"Kip, stop! I swear to God, I'll scream." I blindly reached into my bag and hit the redial button on my phone. If Abby picked up, she'd hear us and call for help.

"Why didn't you believe in me? You and your friends waiting for me to explode like Old Faithful? That's me, one big tourist attraction. Pull over and watch."

"It's not like that!" My arms and back felt like they were about to break. "You can turn this around right now—*we* can turn it around."

He picked me up, and I sighed. But then he grabbed

me by the shoulders and threw me toward the wall. I hit the bureau hard, then fell to the floor.

"I *hate* that you told her." He was crying now. "Couldn't you have had a little more faith?"

By this point, I was too busy making an escape plan to answer. If I kept inching my way across the carpet, I might get to the door before he noticed.

"You bring this out in me—*you*!"

I tried to make eye contact, reach the part of him that didn't want to be doing this.

His eyes were as dead and fearful as mine.

"Kip—"

He hit me again. This time I screamed as loud as I could.

"Oh God, what am I doing?" He pulled me toward him just as the door opened with a kick. A man who looked vaguely familiar grabbed Kip by the shoulders and yanked him off me.

I stared at the man pinning Kip to the bed. I felt like I was going to pass out.

Abby bent over me and screamed, "Call 911!"

It wasn't until Abby dragged me into the bathroom that I realized who the shirtless man with the bald head and the bike shorts was.

"Delilah."

But he was all business, telling 911 to send a police car and an ambulance.

When Kip protested, Delilah put his knee in Kip's back to keep him on the bed. Abby helped me stand up; I cried even harder when I caught my reflection in the mirror.

"It's okay," Abby said through her own tears.

Kip winced on the bed. "Please, let me help."

"I don't think so," Delilah said.

"You're hurting me!" Kip yelled.

"Not nearly enough," Delilah answered.

Abby washed my face with the towels.

I could barely speak through my sobs. "Did you get my call?"

"Yeah, when we were pulling into the parking lot."

"I'm sorry I lied to you."

"Ssshh."

"You were right," I continued. "I should have listened."

I touched my cheek; the impression of the carpet burned deep into my face. "The Improv . . ."

Abby held the wet towel to my face. "Looks like Jimmy Fallon's all mine."

We heard the sirens coming down the street. The police cuffed Kip and took him away. He was still crying.

He tried to catch my eye, but Abby shoved me back into the bathroom. After they left, a female cop led me to the ambulance.

Delilah put her arm around my shoulder. "It's a good thing *one* of you has some sense. Abby came pounding on my door, wouldn't even let me put my face on."

"I almost didn't recognize you."

"Honey, I hate to tell you how many times you've passed me on the street when I was coming back from the gym."

Abby climbed into the ambulance with me. Delilah followed in the bus they'd hijacked from the tour's driver.

"You might have to stay," Abby said. "You look pretty bad."

The thought of calling my parents from the hospital brought on a new wave of nausea.

"I'm staying with you," she said. "Forget the Improv."

"Over my dead body."

"Don't even *say* that!"

Abby asked the attendant for a paper bag and took deep breaths into it. She was as upset as I'd ever seen her. "He could have killed you," she said between breaths and tears.

"Believe me, I know."

I threw up into a bucket the attendant quickly slipped beside my gurney.

I tried to block the scene from my mind, but I couldn't. It wasn't the burn of my cheek on the carpet that I kept returning to or the cd's scattered all over the room with my blood, it was the glimmer of fear I'd felt in my gut as Kip unlocked the door.

I was paying the price for not trusting my instincts.

NOTES TO SELF:

Images embedded in my mind forever—
● My father banging his fists on the sink in my
hospital room.
● Mike and Abby sitting on either side of my bed,
trying to pretend the Improv wasn't the best night
of their lives. (To say nothing of Jimmy Fallon—
Abby's new best friend.)
● Mom's hand flying up to her mouth when she
realized Hannah wasn't the one who pulled off my
earring.
● The stewardess eyeing my bruises every time she
walked up the aisle on the flight back.
● The judge hiccupping as she issued the restraining
order.
● My mother and Kip's, both crying outside the
courtroom.

From the Paper Towel Dialogues of
Kip Costello

The scene was unbearable—Becky's face, the cops cuffing me, calling my mother, her trying to find a local attorney.... It was forty-eight hours of living hell.

I know, I know. It was my own fault. Kind of hard to blame it on Becky when she's the one with the two broken ribs. I tried not to let the other guys in the cell see me break down, but when that cop told me about how hurt she was, I couldn't hold back. I had pictured myself so many times stepping off that cycle of violence we talk about in group. But there's a big difference between <u>knowing</u> what you're supposed to do and <u>doing</u> it. The facilitator sounded let-down when he finally got me on the phone. And Mom . . . I can't even go there.

Forty sessions, two hours each. I used to be one of the guys in group who came on his own; now I'm one of the court-mandated Neanderthals. I sit in the back, not talking. If I start to look at my own shame, I think it'll smother me. This totally and completely SUCKS.

Mom insisted I continue with the last few weeks of school, with my jobs. When I was setting up the crib for Mrs. Lawton yesterday, she was treating me with such respect and gratitude, I thought I was going to puke. Don't be nice to me. I'm an animal. I don't belong in the same room with you, with anyone. I read this thing the other day at group—experience is what you get when you didn't get what you wanted. All I ever wanted to be was a guy who stood onstage and made people laugh, a guy in a good relationship.

I blew that one.

Well, I guess there's some good news. They say in group that a lot of guys don't really turn it around until they hit bottom. I'm so low, I have to look up to see roadkill.

It's gotta be uphill from here.

Put on the headdress and
the eyeliner, honey—you're
Cleopatra, Queen of Denial.

The burn on my cheek healed.

So did my black eyes.

Eventually my ribs did too.

But those were the easy things.

I still woke up terrified a few nights a week. I replayed that night in my mind—weighing the hope and love against the fear and betrayal. But most of the time I blamed myself. Not just for going to Kip's room but for thinking he could've been "fixed" so quickly.

I analyzed that night more often than a Steven Wright video. I realized each of the times Kip had hit or grabbed me had come when I was trying to leave. It was almost like my leaving was his biggest fear. Yet the way he expressed that fear was what drove me away. I fixated on that Catch-22 for hours on end.

When I thought about it, the emotional and verbal abuse was just as painful as the physical. Remembering all the put-downs and nitpicking I'd endured, I covered my head with my pillow and screamed.

I kept coming back to that lame physics experiment. I remembered what happened when you cut off the centripetal force binding the object to its center—it flew off on a tangent. That was me now, hurtling through space, unmoored from what had been keeping me connected to the rest of the universe for the past eight and a half months.

Since this was Kip's first offense, the prosecutor in Santa Barbara agreed to counseling, a batterer support group, and community service back in San Francisco— the maximum amount of all, thanks to my mother. The restraining order was her idea too; she told me later that Kip had instructed his attorney to okay everything she asked for.

I hadn't seen Kip since that night at the motel a month ago and knew in my bones I wouldn't see him again. I didn't want to either.

~~

Who said it gets worse before it gets better?

They were right.

There were some benefits to the tragedy, of course. Mom quietly agreed when I told her I didn't want to go to graduation. The whole party/prom scene seemed even more surreal than usual, and I wanted to be as far away from the celebration mentality as possible. I watched the tape of the Improv show over and over in some kind of self-punishing ritual. Mike had called several times; both he and Abby had had their calendars filled with gigs since MTV aired the show. Despite my situation, I was happy for them.

Besides, why be on MTV or go to the first prom of your life when you can go to a support group instead? When it came time for the first meeting, I slunk downstairs with my notebook and pen.

My mother was standing by the door with her keys.

"You're coming with me?" I asked.

"Don't I always?"

"This isn't one of my gigs," I said. "You don't have to come."

"If you don't want me to go in, I can just drive you," she said. "How does that sound?"

"It sounds horrible. You know I don't want to go."

She held the door open for me. "You've been through the worst of it," she said. "Believe me."

Mom waited at the coffee shop next door to the community center, the same place where I'd emceed my first talent show. This time the atmosphere was slightly less fun—girls my age, sitting on folding chairs in a circle, sharing their stories of abuse. The rich, preppy girl next to me talked about how numb she still felt, how every time her boyfriend hit her it felt like it was happening to someone else. The Goth next to her talked about how her boyfriend used to pinch and poke her in the halls at school while teachers looked on and did nothing. One honor student who brought her boyfriend up on charges was told by the judge to "get on with her life" while she stood in court with two black eyes and a broken nose. Her boyfriend was released that day.

I sat through the meeting without speaking.

—✦—

Mr. Perez finally okayed the San Francisco murder tour I had suggested last year. *Jagged Edge, D.O.A.,* and *Basic Instinct.* I had made pages of notes, screened each movie twice, but when the time came to muster up some enthusiasm for these thrillers I was not prepared at all. Mr. Perez had to prod me along when I spaced out during my presentation. Afterward, he suggested I take some time off to get ready for school in September. I took him up on his offer.

Back at the tour office, I called my mother and told her I was walking home. Put one foot in front of the other—that's right, you remember how. When I spotted the spires of Grace Cathedral, I decided to stop by.

My father used to take me there when I was young to visit the large labyrinth outside the church. Dad would walk for what seemed like hours, never calling me back from running, just gesturing quietly as he followed the circular path toward the center. Maybe other dads stopped at a bar to calm themselves after work; mine meditated around the labyrinth at Grace Cathedral.

I headed to the entrance and started walking. Slowly, deliberately, taking deep breaths. The repetitive movement calmed my body but barely dented my overactive mind.

I followed the well-worn stone of the labyrinth; maybe if I never stopped, I'd wear down a path to some kind of truth. Other people came and went. I kept walking.

The tremor began slowly, then shook me off the labyrinth. My legs buckled underneath me, and I almost fell. I'd never been outside during an earthquake; it felt like the entire city was being slammed by a giant truck. After a few seconds, it subsided. I stumbled away from the labyrinth and sat on one of the benches.

I looked at the young woman reading next to me. "What do you think?" I asked. "A five or a six?"

"Excuse me?"

"The tremor. You think it was a five?"

She looked at me with a puzzled expression on her face and told me she hadn't felt a thing.

I joked about how engrossing her book must be before the impossible dawned on me—was *I* the one with the tremor? I grabbed my bag and ran toward the gate.

Of course this woman didn't feel anything; she probably didn't let her boyfriend beat her up, probably had more self-esteem than to put herself in danger rather than be alone. She probably knew how to trust her instincts, how to stand up for herself, didn't walk around carrying dead animals in her bag. She looked normal, not some freak with a natural disaster inside her just waiting to be unleashed.

I cried big racking sobs the whole way home.

My emotions were so up and down over the next few weeks, I *could* have registered on the Richter scale. I found myself going to Grace Cathedral often, in a half-baked attempt to make sure the tremors were a one-time thing. I walked for miles every day, staring down at the worn stone. As I walked toward the center, I concentrated on creating my own centripetal force, one that connected me to a better center than Kip. Abby came with me sometimes, saying she could kill two personal goals at the same time—meditating and exercising.

One afternoon as I approached the labyrinth, I looked up to see my father taking thoughtful, silent steps. I stood near one of the benches and watched him for several minutes before he spotted me. I waited as he completed the circuitous path.

"Have you been coming here a lot?" His top lip glistened with sweat.

"Pretty much every day."

He nodded. "Me too."

We sat on a bench and watched an elderly woman navigate the maze with her walker.

In the several weeks since the incident in L.A., my dad and I had barely spoken. He suddenly seemed to be working extra shifts or taking Christopher to play dates and games that Delilah would have normally taken him to. I didn't help matters much either; the guilt of having put my family through this whole ordeal kept me in my room alone more than at the kitchen table with them.

"I'm sorry about what happened," I finally said.

"*You're* sorry? I blame myself, not you."

"You didn't do anything."

Since the abuse had come out in the open, it seemed like all of us were eager to grab as much blame as possible.

"It was all *him*," Dad corrected.

I wondered if it would ever be possible for my father to speak the word *Kip* again.

"I should have been there to protect you."

"You say that about everything that happens. But you can't."

"I know. I know." He rubbed his hands together. "But if I ever see him again, Becky, I swear they'll have to peel him off the curb."

"Those kind of feelings got Kip into this mess, don't you think?"

"That's the scary part. I don't know where to put all this anger either. That's why I'm walking."

It was strange having this conversation with my father. For the past few years, most of our talks had revolved around school or curfews or movies; the violence of my relationship with Kip had catapulted all of us into uncharted emotional territory.

The old woman stood peacefully in the center of the circle. My father looked at me and smiled.

"Now, there's a picture."

I agreed; the woman looked like the center of a fabulous flower.

"We just need to give this some time," he said.

I nodded but kept staring at the woman oblivious to the forces around her.

My father turned to me with a serious expression. "But I do have one question for you."

"Shoot."

"Delilah," he said. "Shaved head? Buzz cut? What?"

I smiled. "Shaved. Really handsome. But much shorter than usual."

He shook his head. "It's those heels." He smiled and pointed toward the labyrinth. "Last time we were here together, I think I carried you on my shoulders."

"Don't get any ideas."

"No, Beck. This time you're on your own."

I smiled and began to carve my own tentative path behind my father's.

∼

When I got to my job at Goodwill a few days later, I noticed large chalk letters on the sidewalk outside the store—I AM SORRY. The letters were a foot tall and purple. I stepped over them without thinking twice.

Outside the diner, I saw the phrase again. This time a bit larger, in yellow. I didn't think the writing had anything to do with me until I saw them at the top of my street and outside the tour office when I picked up my last check. Nah, couldn't be. I pictured other phrases in large, colorful block letters. BECKY—STOP BLAMING YOURSELF. IT WAS ME. I AM COMMITTED TO FIXING THIS. I WILL NOT BOTHER YOU AGAIN. I imagined the letters in their bright pastels written across every sidewalk in the city. But that many words, that many letters still couldn't come close to making sense of what had happened.

I couldn't even console myself with the usual thought a comic has at life's most miserable moments: *Well, at least I can use it in my act.* Being abused was a topic so unfunny and uncomfortable I knew I'd never try to work it into a set. The ambitious part of me resented the fact that I had to suffer without the twisted perk of new material.

Although I knew it was silly to ask why, that was the question that ricocheted through my brain continually. Sure, there were plenty of theories in the books Mom brought home, but nothing that explained how a nice guy like Kip could have gotten so out of control. Or how someone as "smart" as me could have stayed in the relationship with her fingers crossed, hoping for the best in the face of contradictory evidence. It dawned on me that the Kip I was in love with was an imaginary Kip—a thoughtful, loving guy who didn't abuse me. *That* Kip didn't exist. The guy I loved had a problem—a *big* one— and no amount of wishful thinking could change it. I felt too young for such life lessons; I guess the universe felt differently.

Little by little, week by week, I began to open up in the support group. By the tone of shame in the room, you'd think we were the batterers and not the victims. (God, I hate that word. *Both* words.) We talked about how other people blamed us for our situation, thinking we were weak or stupid. And how we felt that way ourselves half the time.

Even my brother, Christopher, had asked why I'd let Kip hit me. My mother dragged him from the room with words like "complicated" and "wrong," leaving the question hanging in the air.

The facilitator spoke about looking toward the future, learning to trust other people again, building up antennae to spot trouble so nothing like this would reoccur.

I wasn't there yet.

But I thought of our group differently now. At first, I looked at our sorry selves as a bunch of losers who constantly made bad decisions, but lately I'd been thinking of us as almost brave.

"Well?" My mother closed her book and looked up at me expectantly.

I took a sip of her coffee and sat down beside her. "I feel a little less dead."

She smiled, one of the few times since she'd burst through the door of the hospital back in Santa Barbara. "That's as good a place as any to start."

Months after the incident, my mother still insisted on bringing home videos about dating violence and domestic abuse instead of normal movies. When I finally talked her into watching a regular movie again, Abby invited herself to sleep over and watch it with us. For the first time, Christopher came up with the idea for the night's feature—*E.T.* cued to Dad's throwback cd *Goodbye Yellow Brick Road*. I had to hand it to him; it was one of the best choices ever.

I woke up in the middle of the night to Abby shaking me. "Get up," she said.

I rolled over and looked at my watch. "It's four o'clock!"

"Come on." She stood by the edge of my bed and handed me my jeans.

I told her I wanted to sleep, not meditate.

"We're not going to the Center. We'll be back in an hour."

I grudgingly got dressed and followed her downstairs.

"Where are the stuffed animals?"

"The what?"

"The dead things."

When I finally understood what she meant, I pointed to the cellar stairs. We tiptoed down to the basement, and I showed her my little zoo.

"You are so Norman Bates. When we watch *Psycho*, we won't need a cd—you can just sing."

"It's too early for jokes. Where are we going?"

She didn't answer me. We put the animals into two large boxes and carried them upstairs.

"I don't want to throw them away," I said.

"Oh, we're not throwing them away. You have to trust me on this."

We left the house quietly and packed everything into the car. I told her I wasn't going anywhere without coffee, so we stopped at the diner for a couple of cups to go.

She told me to park the car a few blocks from the supermarket where she worked.

"Are you going to tell me what we're doing?"

"We're finishing up our community service project, putting a little *aha* into people's day."

She handed me one of the boxes, then took a rabbit's foot keychain from her pocket. (How appropriate.) She unlocked the door to the supermarket.

"I didn't know they let you have a key."

"One of the perks of being an assistant manager."

"Uhm . . . isn't this breaking and entering?"

"I told you, they gave me the key!"

The door slid open, and Abby immediately went to the security alarm. She punched in a code, and the lights stopped blinking. She took two flashlights out of her pocket.

"We have to do this in the dark," she said. "I figure we've got ten minutes max."

"It might help if you tell me what we're doing. . . ."

She shone the flashlight on the boxes of critters. "We're going with our instincts."

It didn't take me long to get the hang of Abby's plan.

Several minutes later, Abby locked the door behind us, and we headed to the car.

On the drive back, I began to panic that my mother had gotten up early and discovered we were gone. After all she'd been through these past few months, I didn't want to worry her further.

"I told your mother last night we might go to the Center for morning meditation." She patted my arm. "Don't worry. I thought of everything."

"Now what do we do, O Mastermind?"

"The store opens at nine. You should come in, do some shopping, wait for the fireworks to start."

"This whole thing doesn't sound very Zen to me."

Abby shrugged. "We like to find the humor in the universe. But sometimes you've got to prod it along."

I dropped her off at the Center and told her I'd meet her at the store later.

I tiptoed back into the house; everyone was still asleep. I got into bed and stared at the collage on my desk. Comedy superstars laughing uproariously at my act. With all the fallout from my relationship with Kip, never feeling funny again was one of the results I feared most. I knew I had to get back on the horse, so to speak, but I couldn't imagine standing onstage for a very long while.

At breakfast, I promised Christopher I would take him to the library later. He had discovered the architecture section and was now obsessed. My father even suggested the two of them design a workshop in the basement. It looked like I had moved my menagerie just in time.

At ten past nine, I wheeled my carriage into the grocery store.

I was feeling the tomatoes for ripeness when the first scream came. It was the next aisle over; a twenty-something woman in jogging gear stood in the center of the soda aisle holding a two-liter bottle and pointing to the rows of Coke.

"There's some kind of animal in there!"

A store employee put down his stamp gun and ran to help her. He moved the bottles aside and screamed too. Soon other customers crowded the aisle, including Mr. Sullivan, the manager. Abby made her way to the front and handed him a broom.

"Mr. Sullivan, will this help?"

He took the broom and poked at the small fox. When it didn't move, he stopped prodding it and looked closer.

"I think it's dead."

"A dead animal is worse!" the woman behind me cried.

"Not *dead,* dead. You know, stuffed."

As the customers gathered closer, another scream came, this time from the baby aisle. A woman was holding a package of Pampers in one hand, a crow in the other. She didn't seem scared, just confused. I hadn't put anything in that part of the store; that one was all Abby.

Next, the party aisle. Two kids were jumping up and down shrieking at the squirrel tucked into the cellophane bags of snacks. Mr. Sullivan raced from aisle to aisle calming down the customers. I sidled up behind Abby while he talked the boys out of playing with the squirrel.

"Do you think anyone gets that the squirrel is with the nuts?" I whispered.

She burst out laughing, then stopped before anyone

saw her. I cruised the aisles waiting for the next discoveries. A man with Birkenstocks and a beard curiously examined the ferret tucked among the jars of tomato sauce. A large crowd gathered around the badger lying contentedly behind the bags of dog food. Two little girls stood in their carriages yelling, "Eek! A mouse!"

Mr. Sullivan locked the doors so no one else could come in. Abby ran down the aisles with the other employees, pretending to root out the animals before the customers found them.

I stood at the front of the store and watched the freak show unfold before me. Over the years I'd been with Abby through several pranks, but this was clearly our masterpiece. No one hurt, no one injured, but everyone AWAKE, you could count on that. When I saw a young boy take the stamp gun and start pricing the raccoon, I laughed until the tears ran down my face. I realized how long it had been since I'd laughed at anything. After a while, I couldn't tell if I was laughing or crying, but it didn't really matter.

Mr. Sullivan finally booted everyone out of the store until he could be assured there were no more animals. (I hate to tell you, Mr. S., but you're not going to find the weasel for weeks—trust me on this.)

When I stopped laughing and made it to the sidewalk, I noticed a woman carrying a small opossum under each arm. She was trying to hail a cab. As Abby ushered the other customers to the curb, she spotted her too.

"Are you thinking what I'm thinking?" I asked.

"She's all yours."

I approached the woman and asked if I could help her. I held up my arm to call a cab.

"Taxi!"

Abby came up beside me. "Dermy!"

"Taxi!"

"Dermy!"

The woman had no idea what we were talking about, which made the whole thing that much funnier. She took off down the street with her prized catch.

When Abby headed back inside, I grabbed her by the arm.

"Thank you," I said.

"What are you talking about? I didn't do this for you."

"You're lying, but thanks anyway."

She placed her hands in front of her heart and bowed. "Community service Zen project is now officially over."

I hung around on the sidewalk for a while; it was fun to hear the buzz surrounding our little performance art. I broke out laughing several times as the events replayed themselves in my mind.

And when I headed back home, I felt better than I had in months.

A key, a jar, lightning.

Gotcha!

NOTES TO SELF:

● Try to get back to normal with Delilah—it still seems weird that I saw her out of costume. I've been thinking about this a lot—it's almost like I was the female impersonator, not Delilah. The way I tried to be this perfect girlfriend for Kip—more fictional than anyone Delilah's ever tried to be.

● Poor Christopher's been following me around like a puppy. I need to hang out with him more before I leave for school.

● Mr. Perez suggested working for his sister company in L.A. if I need extra money—Chinatown, here we come.

● I'm not in love with him, almost don't miss him anymore. But I do think about Kip and wonder if he's okay.

● I should've at least kept the squirrel.

From the Paper Towel Dialogues of
Kip Costello

Got my two-month pin today. Maybe I'll have Mom pick up one of those Boy Scout sashes at a yard sale, fill it up with pins one month at a time. Maybe I'll start wearing it onstage—my new trademark—BE PREPARED.

I wasn't prepared for that girl to start chatting me up after my gig in Palo Alto last night. Boy, did I finish my drink and run. The last thing I need right now is to start dating. Even a slow learner like me realizes what a recipe for disaster <u>that</u> would be. . . .

Becky. I miss making her laugh, miss holding her, miss pretty much everything about her. I saw her and Abby leaving the diner last week—I almost jumped into the bushes so she wouldn't think I was stalking her (which I wasn't). I hope she got the chalk messages. I didn't know what else to do, as if words—in chalk, no less—could ever come close to letting her know how sorry I am.

Her hair's starting to grow out; I actually like it now. I hope she enjoys UCLA and gets some gigs down there. I caught the Improv rerun on MTV—it slayed me to see her friends kicking ass and not her.

I tried out my new set last night—the whole we're-all-trying-to-be-tough-guys thing—and it went over well. I really connected, could see the wheels turning while the audience listened. At one point, I was laughing along with them, making myself laugh at the same time, and God knows that doesn't happen often enough.

Mrs. Lawton's granddaughter loved the room; I'm glad. When she introduced me to Katie, Mrs. Lawton told her what a "nice boy" I was. I had to bite my lip to stop from blubbering all over the carpet. Maybe it's the support group, maybe it's time, but I think about the relationship so much differently now. I used to blame Becky for most everything that was wrong, and didn't really look at how my own actions contributed. I used to be able to justify every destructive action I took. I can see it now.

I repeated the support group checklist like a mantra the whole way home from Mrs. Lawton's. I _am_ going to be a decent guy and will do whatever it takes to be one. I just never realized it was going to be so much work.

I decided to get rid of all my paper towels last night. Sure, there was some good material there, but for every good joke there was a blurb about Becky that sounded so controlling, it made me want to throw all twenty rolls out the window. My mom brought up a big wicker basket from the shop, and we tossed the rolls in like kids playing Nerfball. When I picked up the basket to bring it downstairs, she made some quip about getting rid of dirty laundry. I turned around to give her grief about such a lame joke, but she looked so hopeful, all I could do was smile back at her. God, she's been through hell.

Thought of Becky again last week. There was some snippet in the paper about all these taxidermy animals let loose in a supermarket downtown. Becky would have <u>loved</u> that.

Next time someone offers me a drink at the fountain of knowledge, I'm going to use more than a shot glass.

When it finally came time to drive to L.A. with my family and a U-Haul, I was more than ready for the change. All the focus on me and healing and support—can I please get out of the spotlight so you can pay attention to Christopher for a while?

Abby and I traded our favorite shirts, went to two movies, and each bought a pair of shoes on our last Saturday together. On Sunday, we decorated the room in her new apartment, which she shared with three other girls. She promised to come down within a month to visit.

But Delilah was the one it was tough saying good-bye to. She gave me a box of Uncle Danny's things to take with me, then pretended she had an appointment downtown so she wouldn't be there for the big farewell in the driveway. For someone as theatrical as Delilah, good-bye was still one scene she hated to play.

I'd have given fifty lifetimes to erase the worried expressions on my parents' faces as they helped me unpack in my dorm room. I reassured my mom over and over that

I'd be fine. She nodded and swallowed hard, hoping that would be the case. I knew what it was like to be on the back side of all that hope; I didn't want to let her down.

Before they left, I took a walk with my mom to Health Services. I led her to the bulletin board we'd seen on our first trip there last January. I pointed to the card with the Dating Violence Support Group.

"I promise you I'll go to meetings," I said.

"I want more than that. I want you to promise that if you're ever within fifty feet of another dangerous situation, I'm the first one you call."

"I can do that."

My dad—such a mushball—cried when they got ready to leave. One thing I realized in my bones now: when something happened to one person in the family, it happened to everyone. I owed it to all of us to keep it together. I told my dad we'd walk the labyrinth when I came home in November.

He handed me a business card with the phone number of the best restaurant in L.A. "I used to work with Douglas, the chef. You call him anytime, he'll take care of you. This place may be the restaurant to the stars, but no matter how crowded it is, you'll always have a fine meal there, gratis."

Good old Dad, communicating the best way he knew how, with food.

Christopher handed me an elaborate drawing he'd been working on with a design layout for my dorm room. (I'd given him a drafting set as my going-away present; I think it changed his life.) I picked him up, sat him on the hood of the car, and hugged him hard. I was going to *miss* this little guy.

My mother handed me an envelope. Inside was a passbook to a local bank. The account was filled with several hundred dollars.

"Money for incidentals," she said. "Call if you need more."

"I've been begging for spending money my entire life—I leave the house, *now* you fork it over?"

"You want to come home, I'll have a ticket waiting for you at the airport the same day. If not, we'll see you Thanksgiving." She tied her scarf around her head as she climbed into the car. "But don't even think about coming home if you haven't performed. You get back onstage—pronto. That's an order."

Mom—part mother, part foreman. I waved at the back of the car much longer than they were able to see me.

~

When I returned to the dorm, my new roommate was there. She had a row of silver studs running up both ears, a nose ring, tongue and eyebrow studs, and a leather jacket with dozens of pins. She tore off her Discman and shook my hand.

"Helen Talbot," she said. "Nice to meet you."

I loved the juxtaposition of the punk clothes and the preppy name. If I ever got onstage again, I'd work it into a routine.

"Hope you don't mind, but I went through your music. I was petrified I was going to have to live with some rabid Dave Matthews fan." She held up one of my cd's from the shelf. "I can't believe you have 'Wichi Tai To'! It is absolutely my favorite song of all time."

I looked at the cd in her hands—the anniversary compilation from Kip. I told her that song had been one of my old boyfriend's favorites.

"Old boyfriend, huh? Didn't work out?"

"It ended kind of badly," I answered.

"He might have been the biggest jerk in the world, but anyone who likes *this* song can't be all bad."

"He wasn't all bad. It's one of the reasons it took me so long to leave."

She put the headphones over my ears and turned up the volume. I sat back on my bed and listened to the song Kip used to sing around the house, down the street, always with a smile on his face. It was a great song. For the first time in ages, I felt enough distance from Kip to be able to enjoy it on my own.

Helen and I spent the afternoon sharing our favorite music. After that, she gave me an impromptu fashion show of her piercings and tattoos.

"What's the matter?" she asked. "You don't like to wear earrings?"

I told her I hadn't worn them in a while and that my holes had closed up. I stuck with the Hannah story, not wanting to get into the whole thing with Kip.

She examined my earlobe. "You want me to pierce it again?"

The doctor had said it would be okay to pierce my ear again a few months after it healed. Doing that suddenly seemed necessary, even important. Helen borrowed some ice from a student down the hall with a fridge, then took out a little suede pouch full of needles. She sterilized one with some alcohol. I winced when she slipped it into my ear.

She took a post from her own ear, sterilized it, and inserted it into the new hole.

"Just keep it in for a while," she said. "Tomorrow it'll be as good as new."

As I looked at my reddened lobe in the mirror, I felt like my freshman year might actually be starting off well.

～

Registration was the nightmare everyone said it would be; even with waking up pre-dawn—which made me miss Abby desperately—I was shut out of every class I wanted. Comedy writing, full. History of comedy, full. Writing for television, full.

This is how the universe screws around with you; this is how the world drags you kicking and screaming toward your fate.

The only class remotely associated with comedy that had any seats left was Improvisation. I imagined the smile broadening on Abby's face as she sat on her meditation cushion four hundred miles away.

On the first day, I sat in the back of the room and hid behind my notebook. The teacher had a blond pageboy and dressed all in black—surprise, surprise. I figured it was the first class; we were safe.

I was wrong.

She made us write down random words on pieces of paper, which she proceeded to collect in an old hat. (Was this college or kindergarten?) She then took out the class list.

The first name she called was mine.

When I heard the words "Becky Martin" it reminded me of Rick introducing me at the club.

"Becky Martin," she repeated. "Take the stage."

I told her I didn't have anything prepared.

She looked at me as if I'd just said the stupidest thing possible.

"This is an improv class. Of course you don't have anything prepared." She clapped her hands. "Let's go."

As I walked past the rows of other students to the front of the auditorium, I tried to concentrate on my breathing. Difficult to do when you're terrified.

She stood in front of me and held out the hat. I picked a scrap of paper with the word "car." I looked at her expectantly.

"No instructions, no directions. Give me five minutes on your topic." She pointed to the stage. "Go."

Car—brilliant! I could use my whole getting-your-license set. I hadn't practiced it in a while, but even if I forgot some of it, I had a solid five minutes.

I climbed the stairs, then stopped. What if I *didn't* go with my planned set? This was supposed to be improvisation, after all. What if I trusted my instincts, *really* trusted them this time. What would I come up with then?

"Ms. Martin, get a move on before I decide to grade you."

I took the stage.

I had been through hell this past year, through emotional and physical betrayal I never could have imagined. I had survived. I'd stood in front of girls I didn't know and bared my innermost feelings of fear and shame. It seemed silly to be afraid now, especially when I had such important stories to tell. It was time to pry loose the fear and move on.

WHERE ARE YOU?

I am here.

WHO ARE YOU?

Someone who lands on her feet.

I took a deep breath and began.

"My uncle Danny died when I was four. He left me his copy of The Canterbury Tales, *his* Beverly Hillbillies *memorabilia, and an old Toyota to save till I turned sixteen. And his friend Delilah—I inherited her too."*

I looked up just in time to see a guy in the front row yawn.

But the guy next to him held my eye; he was listening, waiting for more. It was about all the give-and-take I could handle right now, but that was fine. Maybe that's the best I could do, connect with the audience one person at a time. I thought of the sign over my desk back home: IF LIFE GIVES IT TO YOU, USE IT. For once, it applied to so much more than comedy. I was creating a body of work; we all were. A lifetime of experiences to absorb, integrate, then move on from. Over time, I would transform the pain of my relationship with Kip into something positive.

When I glanced at the teacher she was looking at me expectantly but with a smile. I'd learn to make the stage feel like home again, crafting jokes word by word, line by line. I would let the laughter heal me.

In the meantime?

I had an audience in front of me, waiting to connect.

A Note from the Author

I was reading Naomi Wolf's *Promiscuities,* in which she talks about being physically abused by her boyfriend while in high school. I was shocked; if a leading feminist—a strong young woman from an educated family— was being beaten by her boyfriend, what chances did the average girl have? The very next day (I love coincidences) Harvard released a study in the *Journal of the American Medical Association* stating that "one out of every five" teenage girls gets physically abused by her boyfriend. When I talked to professionals about these statistics, most thought they were low. I knew then that this was a topic I wanted to write about.

It didn't interest me, however, to show a relationship in black-and-white terms. In Wolf's book, she describes her boyfriend as a nice guy most of the time. This is one of the reasons why it becomes so difficult for girls and women to leave. I wanted to write a novel that showed how easily we blame the victim for the situation she's in.

I also wanted to show *both* parties dealing with the issue of abuse. As much as Kip's actions are horrendous, he is struggling with his behavior too. Demonizing the perpetrator hardly begins to fix such a complicated problem. For me, it made more sense to try and understand him.

In our culture, boys and men swim against a rushing tide of violence; girls and women often bear the brunt of their frustration and rage. Helping both parties heal themselves means eliminating violence in our society by its roots.

We have a lot of work to do.

Acknowledgments

A humble and grateful thank-you to the young women and men who shared their stories with me. Thanks to Mike Nakkula and the others at the Risk Prevention Program at the Harvard Graduate School of Education. Special thanks also to Russell Bradbury-Carlin and Steve Jefferson at the Men's Resource Center of Western Massachusetts and MOVE for their information and honesty. Any students who haven't seen the educational video *Tough Guise* should ask their schools to order it immediately. Also, the National Domestic Violence Hotline (800-799-SAFE) fields calls from teens twenty-four hours a day. On a lighter note, big thanks to Marianne Leone and Ray Ellin for their comedic talents, as well as to several Internet public domain joke sites. Ditto to Judith Souza and Liz Miller, my two favorite reasons for loving San Francisco. And to Mark Morelli, for twenty-five years of generosity, photos, and friendship.